Harlequin Romance®

2933
2.25

The Course of True Love

Betty Neels

This
Harlequin Romance

*belongs in the
personal library of*

_____

"Will you miss me?" Marc asked Claribel

He was returning to Holland the following week. Claribel hesitated, then said, "Well, yes, I think I shall."

"But you will doubtless have many dates."

"Yes, but they're not like you," she said honestly.

"You must have had offers of marriage?" he said.

Claribel realized the wine she had drunk was loosening her tongue, so she decided to turn the tables rather than continue to respond to Marc's strange, personal probings. "Are *you* going to get married, Mr. van Borsale?"

He smiled a little. "Yes, I plan to settle down and become a family man."

"In Holland, of course?" Claribel dreaded his answer, and when it came, her heart fell like a stone.

"Of course," he said.

"I hope you will be very happy," was all the distraught Claribel could say.

Betty Neels is well-known for her romances set in the Netherlands, which is hardly surprising. She married a Dutchman and spent the first twelve years of their marriage living in Holland and working as a nurse. Today she and her husband make their home in a small ancient stone cottage in England's West Country, but they return to Holland often. She loves to explore tiny villages and tour privately owned homes there, in order to lend an air of authenticity to the background of her books.

Books by Betty Neels

HARLEQUIN ROMANCE

Don't miss any of our special offers. Write to us at the following address for information on our newest releases.

Harlequin Reader Service
901 Fuhrmann Blvd., P.O. Box 1397, Buffalo, NY 14240
Canadian address: P.O. Box 603,
Fort Erie, Ont. L2A 5X3

The Course of True Love

Betty Neels

Harlequin Books

TORONTO • NEW YORK • LONDON
AMSTERDAM • PARIS • SYDNEY • HAMBURG
STOCKHOLM • ATHENS • TOKYO • MILAN

Original hardcover edition published in 1988
by Mills & Boon Limited

ISBN 0-373-02933-0

Harlequin Romance first edition September 1988

CHAPTER ONE

MARCH was doing exactly as it should; it had come in like a lamb, now it was going out like a lion. An icy rain driven by a roaring wind was sweeping the streets clear of all but those unfortunates who had been forced to go out. And these, needless to say, were scuttling along, anxious to get within doors as fast as possible.

There was a long queue half-way down the street, an impatient line of people under umbrellas, jostling for position, ready to rush forward when their bus arrived. The girl at the end of the queue edged away from the drips running down the back of her neck from the umbrella behind her and sighed resignedly. It had been a long day and she was tired and home was still a bus ride away; she could not even tell if she would be lucky enough to get on to the next bus . . .

It came, sending great splashes of water from the gutter as it slowed to a halt. The queue surged forward. The owner of the umbrella gave her a vicious poke in the back as the slow-moving elderly man in front of her stepped back and planted a foot on her instep. She gave a gasp of pain and came to an involuntary halt, to be instantly swept aside by those behind her. Which meant one foot, the injured one, in the muddy water of the gutter.

The bus went, taking with it almost all the queue, leaving the girl to lift a dripping foot back on to the pavement and

hobble to join it once more. But she didn't reach it; the car
which had drawn up behind the bus edged forward and
stopped beside her and the driver got out.

He looked even taller than he actually was in the light of
the street lamps and she couldn't see him very clearly. He
said with decided impatience, 'Are you hurt? I saw what
happened. Get into the car, I'll drive you home.'

She looked up from the contemplation of torn tights and a
trickle of blood. 'Thank you; I prefer to go by bus.' Her
voice was a pretty as her face but there was a decided chill
to it.

'Don't be a fool, young woman, I've no intention of
kidnapping you. Besides, you look hefty enough to take care
of yourself.' He ignored her outraged gasp. 'Don't keep me
waiting, I have an appointment.' The impatience was even
more decided.

Still smarting from having her Junoesque and charming
person referred to as hefty, the girl took his proffered arm
and allowed herself to be settled beside him. 'Where to?' he
asked, and slid into the stream of traffic.

The girl gave a delicate sniff; the car was a Rolls-Royce
and smelled of leather and, faintly, of cologne. She said in
her nice voice, still chilly though, 'You should have asked
me before I got into the car, which I wouldn't have done if
you hadn't been so impatient. Meadow Road, a turning off
Stamford Street. That's . . .'

'I know where it is. Which number?'

'Fifteen.' She added, 'It's quite a long way. You could
drop me off at a bus-stop; I shall be quite all right.'

He didn't answer, and after a moment she realised that he
wasn't going to. She glanced at her foot; it had left a
muddy, watery mark on the car's splendid carpet and it

was bleeding sluggishly. Nothing serious, she decided.

They crossed the river and he turned the car into the busy streets around Waterloo station and then, without being told, into Meadow Road, a dingy street which didn't live up to its name for there wasn't a blade of grass throughout its length. Its houses were bay-windowed with steps leading to shabby front doors, and iron railings concealed the semi-basements. Her companion stopped before number fifteen and got out. It surprised her when he opened her door and offered a hand. She stood on the pavement, looking up at him; she was a tall girl but she had to look quite a way.

'Thank you, you were most kind. I hope you won't be late for your appointment.'

'What is your name?'

She answered matter-of-factly, 'Claribel Brown. What's yours?'

'Marc van Borsele. And now that we are introduced, I will come in with you and see to that foot.'

She saw then that he held a case in one hand. 'You're a doctor?'

'Yes.'

There seemed no point in arguing with him. 'Very well, though I'm perfectly able . . .'

'Let us waste no more time in polite chat.'

Claribel opened the gate to the basement with rather more force than necessary and led the way down the worn steps to her front door. In the sombre light of the street lamp its paint shone in a vibrant red and there were tubs on either side, holding the hopeful green shoots of daffodils. She got out her key and had it taken from her and the door opened. He switched on the light, too, and then stood aside for her to enter.

There was a tiny lobby and an inner door leading to the living-room, small and perforce dark but very cosy. The furniture was mostly second-hand but had been chosen with care, and there was an out-of-date gas fire under the narrow mantelshelf. The one easy chair was occupied by two cats, one black and white, one ginger, curled up together. They unrolled themselves as Claribel went in, muttered softly at her, and curled up again.

'Do come in,' said Claribel unnecessarily, for he was already right behind her.

They stood for a moment and studied each other. Claribel was a pretty girl, almost beautiful with golden hair drawn back rather too severely into a knot, green eyes and a straight nose above a generous mouth. She was tall and magnificently built and looked a good deal younger than her twenty-eight years.

She stared back at her companion, frowning faintly because he was staring even harder. He was well over six feet, she supposed, and big with huge shoulders. He was also good-looking in a formidable way, with dark hair, sprinkled with grey, an aggressive nose, a firm thin mouth and dark eyes. He might be any age between thirty-five and forty, she guessed, and he had a nice taste in dress: conservative but elegant.

'Be good enough to take off your tights or whatever and let me see that foot.' He glanced at his watch. 'I can spare five minutes.'

The arrogance of the man! Someone should take him in hand, Claribel thought as he turned to undo his case. She whipped off her tights, sat down on a small upright chair and held her foot out.

There was more mud and blood; he poked and prodded,

remarked that she would have a bruised foot but nothing worse and suggested that she should wash it. 'That's if you have a bathroom?'

She bit back what she would liked to have said in reply and went through the door at the back of the room and shut it behind her. The bathroom was a pokey little place reached through her bedroom; she cleaned her foot and whisked back to find him standing before the watercolour hanging over the mantelpiece.

'Your home?' he wanted to know.

'Yes.'

'The west country?'

'Yes.' She had sat down and was holding her foot once more. 'You said you had five minutes . . .'

He sat on his heels, used penicillin powder, gauze and strapping and then stood up. 'You don't like me,' he observed.

'I don't know you. Thank you for your help. You were kind.'

'I am not a particularly kind man.' He closed his case and she opened the door and held out a nicely kept hand.

'Goodbye, Dr van Borsele.'

He shook it briefly. 'Goodbye. You live alone?'

She was surprised. 'Yes. Well, there are Enoch and Toots . . .'

'I trust that you don't open your door to strangers or accept lifts from those you don't know.'

Her pretty mouth dropped open. 'Well! You insisted on bringing me home and here you are telling me . . .' She strove to keep her voice at a reasonable level. 'I never accept lifts and I certainly don't open my door. Whatever do you take me for?'

'The most beautiful girl I have seen for a long time.' He didn't smile. 'Goodnight, Claribel.'

She bolted the door after him and stood listening to him driving away.

'What an extraordinary man,' she observed to her cats, 'and much too sure of himself.'

She went into the kitchenette and began to get her supper, all the while considering ways and means of deflating his arrogance. 'I dare say he's quite nice,' she mused out loud, 'once one gets beneath that cold manner. Perhaps he is crossed in love. Or unhappily married. And what's he doing here in London if he's Dutch?'

She dished up her omelette and sat down at the table in the living-room to eat it. 'I wonder what he does? Private practice, or just on a visit, or at one of the hospitals?'

She finished her supper, fed the cats and washed up, turned on the gas fire and got out the sweater she was knitting, but somehow she couldn't settle to it. Presently she bundled it up and took herself off to bed, where, to her annoyance, she lay awake thinking, much against her will, of the man she had met that evening. 'A good thing we'll not meet again,' she observed to the cats curled up on the end of her bed, 'for he's too unsettling.'

It was still raining when she got up the next morning, dressed, breakfasted, fed the cats and tidied up her small flat. The physiotherapy department opened at nine o'clock and Miss Flute, who was in charge, had put her down to do a ward round with Mr Shutter, the orthopaedic consultant, at half past that hour. She needed to go through the notes before then.

The bus was jammed with damp passengers, irritable at that hour of the morning. Claribel wedged herself between a staid city gent and a young girl with purple hair arranged in spikes, and reviewed the day before her.

A busy one. Mr Shutter had the energy of two men and expected everyone to feel the same way; she had no doubt that by the end of his round she would have added more patients to the already overfull list Miss Flute brooded over each morning. Besides that, she had several patients of her own to deal with before lunch, and in the afternoon Mr Shutter had his out-patients clinic. It crossed her mind that she had more than her fair share of that gentleman; there were, after all, four other full-time physiotherapists as well as several who came in part-time. There were other consultants, too, milder, slower men that Mr Shutter, but somehow she always had him. Not that she minded; he was a youngish man, an out-of-doors type whose energy was very much in contrast to his broken-limbed patients, but he was kind to them and she had never minded his heartiness. Some of the girls she worked with found him intimidating, but it had never bothered her; she had a peppery man of the law for a father.

Jerome's Hospital was old; it had been patched up from time to time and there were plans afoot to move it, lock, stock and barrel, to the outskirts of London, but the plans had been mooted so often, and just as often tidied away again, that it seemed likely to stay where it was, surrounded by its dingy streets, its walls grimed from the traffic which never ceased around it, its interior a maze of passages, splendid public rooms and inconvenient wards. Claribel, who had trained there and stayed on afterwards, surveyed its grim exterior as she got off the bus with a mixture of intense dislike and affection. She loved her work, she liked the patients and the people she worked with, but she

deplored the endless corridors, the dimness of the various
departments and the many annexes where it was so easy to
get lost. Her kind heart went out to patients who, for the
first time, arrived for treatment and wandered in
bewilderment all over the place, despite the little signposts
none of them ever saw, until someone took pity on them
and showed them the way, to arrive, hot and flustered, late
for their appointment.

Claribel wished the porter on duty a good morning and
went down the short staircase at the back of the entrance
hall. It led to a narrow passage used by the electricians,
porters and those going to the theatre serving casualty; it
was also a short cut to the physio department. She opened
the door and went in with five minutes to spare.

Miss Flute was already there, a middle-aged, grey-haired
lady with a sharp tongue and a soft heart who led her team
with unflagging energy and didn't suffer fools gladly. She
smiled at Claribel as she wished her a brisk good morning.
'A busy day,' she observed. 'There's a huge out-patients.'

Claribel paused on her way to the cloakroom they all
shared. 'Are we all here?' she asked.

'No. Mrs Green phoned to say that she had a bad
cold—we'll have to share out her patients.'

Claribel got into her white overall, gave her reflection a
perfunctory glance and went into the office to con the notes.
It was indeed going to be a busy day.

The orthopaedic wing was right at the other end of the
hospital and Mr Shutter was doing his rounds in both the
men's and women's wards. Claribel poked her pretty head
round Sister's office door, announced her arrival and joined
the social worker, a nurse burdened with charts and, at the
last minute, Sister herself. Just in time, the ward

doors swung open and Mr Shutter strode in, bringing with him a great rush of energy and fresh air. Also with him was the man who had given Claribel a lift on the previous evening.

Although she had thought about him a great deal, she hadn't expected to see him again, but if she had she would have expected him to at least give some sign of recognition. As it was, his dark eyes looked right through her. She was conscious of annoyance. Of course, it wouldn't have done at all to have spoken to her, but he could have smiled . . .

She took her place in the group surrounding Mr Shutter and the round started. There were sixteen patients in the ward but not all of them were having physio. It wasn't until they reached the fourth bed that Mr Shutter said, 'Claribel, how's this leg shaping? Is it going to need much more massage? It looks pretty good to me.' He glanced at the man beside him.

'What do you think, Marc?' He didn't wait for an answer. 'This is one of our physiotherapists, Claribel Brown. Claribel, Mr van Borsele has joined us for a period—he'll be taking over for a week or two while I'm away. Well, what do you think, Marc?' Mr van Borsele had barely glanced at her; only by the slight nod of his handsome head had he acknowledged that she was there. He studied the limb at some length, smiled nicely at the young man lying in the bed and said, 'Might Miss Brown put this lad through his paces? There's considerable muscle wastage.'

He and Mr Shutter studied the X-rays and they watched Claribel as she exercised the boy's fractured leg; it had been taken out of the plaster, the pin taken from the knee and the extension removed only days before, but thanks to her daily visits there was quite a lot of movement. Of course there was muscle wastage, she reflected silently. If Mr van Borsele should ever break one of his legs and she had the task of exercising it . . . She looked up to catch his dark eyes upon her and a knowing light smile curled his lip. So he read people's thoughts, too, did he?

By a great effort of will she managed not to blush.

The round wound to a close and presently she was able to leave the ward, armed with a great many instructions, and make her way back to the physio department. The waiting-room was full but it always was: people waiting patiently for their turn, holding crutches or walking aids, nursing arms in slings. She uttered a general good morning and went through to the office where Miss Flute was on the phone—admonishing someone severely by the sound of it. She put the receiver down and remarked, 'I have very little patience with some people. Well, I suppose you've collected another bunch of patients. Your Mrs Snow is waiting.' She studied Claribel's face. 'Have a cup of coffee first. Heaven knows when you'll get another chance.'

Claribel sipped thankfully. 'Five more—two discharges to come here three times a week and three on the ward—all extensions. There's a new man taking over from Mr Shutter—did you know?'

'Met him yesterday. Dutch—well thought of, I believe. A bit terse, I thought.'

Claribel put down her empty mug. 'I'll say. Mr Shutter introduced us; he looked right through me.'

Miss Flute said drily, 'How could that be possible?'

Claribel frowned. She was a sensible girl, aware that she had more than her share of good looks, and she was accustomed to people remarking on that, but she had no vanity and was quite uncaring of the admiring glances she drew. All the same, for some reason Mr van Borsele's lack of interest in her had irked her. 'Perhaps he hates blondes . . . or he's a misogynist.'

Miss Flute gave a hoot of laughter. 'My dear girl, the grapevine has it that he is out and about at all the best restaurants with various lovelies.'

'Good luck to him,' said Claribel and went off in search of Mrs Snow. Mrs Snow was elderly, stout and chatty; Claribel rather liked her. She had tripped in her own kitchen and broken an arm and, having passed through Casualty, X-ray and Mr Shutter's Out-patients, was now in the hands of the physio department. She was a chatty soul and at each session related an instalment of her home life while Claribel massaged her and egged her on to do the exercises she was so loath to do.

'I seen a nice young man as I come in,' she observed as Claribel began on the arm. 'Getting out of 'is car, 'e was—one of them Rolls, ever so posh. 'E went into Out-patients.'

She fixed Claribel with a beady eye; having set a sprat to catch a mackerel, she was hopeful of a good catch.

'He's taking over from Mr Shutter for a week or two. You're due to see him next week, aren't you? Mr Shutter is having a holiday.'

''E deserves it. 'E must be sick ter death of other people's bones.' Mrs Snow cringed away from Claribel's gentle fingers. 'Ow, that 'urts. Is 'e nice, the new man?'

'I'm sure he will be very good at his job,' said Claribel sedately. 'Now, Mrs Snow, let me see you lift that arm.'

The day wore on with its unending stream of patients. By five o'clock Claribel was bone-weary. Not that she minded; she liked her work and it was satisfying to see arms and legs returned to normal. Of course there was a hard core of elderlies with arthritis who were more or less permanently on the books, but they still benefited, even if they made little progress.

There was a general rush to go home once the last patient had gone, and a good deal of cheerful chatter since it was Friday and the department closed down until Monday morning. They left in a cheerful bunch, pausing to say goodbye to Miss Flute as she got into her Mini and then streaming across the hospital forecourt, intent on getting their various buses. Claribel, intent on getting home for the weekend, raced away to the nearest bus stop, her mind already dwelling happily on the peace and quiet of her parents' home in Wiltshire, so that she failed to see Mr van Borsele's Rolls at the entrance, waiting to join the rush of traffic in the street. She had in fact forgotten all about him.

She went home once a month, an undertaking which called for a strict routine the moment she got into her flat. Shower and change, feed the cats, stow them in their travelling basket, snatch up her already packed weekend bag and get a taxi, not always easy, especially in her unfashionable corner of London. Waterloo station wasn't all that distance away, but too far to walk with the cats and her bag, and this evening she was later than usual.

She reached the end of Meadow Road and not a taxi in sight, although there was more chance of one in Stamford Street. She paused on the corner by the few rather tatty shops and looked hopefully in either direction. Traffic streamed past but every taxi was occupied; she would have to try for a bus if one came along, although the nearest stop to the station was several minutes away from the station itself.

She didn't see the Rolls, going the other way, slow, do a U-turn and slide to a halt beside her.

'Get in quickly,' begged Mr van Borsele, 'I'm breaking any number of regulations.' He had nipped out smartly, taken the basket from her and put it on the back seat, and hurried her round the car into the seat beside his. 'Where to?'

Claribel caught her breath. 'Waterloo Station. My goodness, you do pop up in unexpected places, don't you?' She added quickly, like a small girl who had forgotten her manners, 'Thank you very much. I haven't much time to catch my train.'

Mr van Borsele grunted and joined the steady stream of traffic, weaving in and out of slower vehicles in a rather unnerving fashion.

'You're going very fast,' Claribel pointed out severely.

He said irritably, 'I was under the impression that you wished to catch a train, or was that just an excuse to get a lift?'

Claribel drew such a deep breath she almost exploded. 'Well, of all the nerve . . .' She remembered suddenly to whom she was speaking; one showed a proper respect towards consultant surgeons. 'You stopped the car and told me to get in.'

'Indeed I did. I don't remember inviting you to criticise my driving.'

She gave his unfriendly profile an almost motherly look. He was touchy; had a tiff with his girlfriend, perhaps. With a brother only a few years younger than herself she was familiar with the sudden snappish reply.

She said reasonably, 'I'm not criticising you at all, Mr van Borsele—I'm very grateful to you.'

He grunted again. Hardly a sparkling conversationalist, she reflected, and prepared to get out as he pulled in at the station's main entrance. She still had almost ten minutes but there would be a queue for tickets. She had a hand on the door handle when he said, 'Wait,' and got out and opened the door, retrieving the cats and her bag from the back of the car and strode into the station. Outside the vast ticket office he asked, 'Where to?'

'Oh, Tisbury.' She put out a hand for the basket and her bag and found she was holding them both and watching his vast back disappearing into the queue. Her protesting, 'Mr van Borsele,' fell on deaf ears.

He was back within five minutes, which left three minutes to get on to the train. He took the cats and her bag from her, bustled her past the platform gate, found her an empty seat opposite two respectable matrons, put the cats on the floor beside her with her bag on the rack, wished her a coldly polite goodbye and had gone while she was on the point of thanking him yet again. She remembered then that he had paid for her ticket and she had forgotten to repay him. What must he think of her? She went pink at the thought and the matrons eyed her with interest, no doubt scenting romance.

She would have to pay him when she got back on Monday; better still, she could put the money in the consultant's letter rack with a polite note. Not that he deserved any politeness. Not a man to do things by halves, she mused as the train gathered speed between the rows of smoke-grimed houses; she had been handled as efficiently as an express parcel. And with about as much interest.

She occupied the train journey composing cool observations to Mr van Borsele when next they met, calculated to take him down a peg.

Less than two hours later she was on the platform at Tisbury station being hugged by her father and then hurried to the family car, an elderly estate car in constant use, for he was a solicitor of no mean repute and much in demand around the outlying farms and small estates. Enoch and Toots were settled in the back with Rover, the family labrador, and Mr Brown, without loss of time, drove home.

His family had lived in the same house for some considerable time. It was a typical dwelling of the district: mellowed red brick, an ancient slate roof and plenty of ground round it. A roomy place, with a stable converted to a garage and a couple of rather tumbledown sheds to one side, it stood a mile outside the little town, its garden well tended. It had never had a name but was known locally as Brown's place.

Its owner shot up the short drive and Claribel jumped out to fling open the door and hurry inside, leaving her father to bring in the animals. Mrs Brown came out of the kitchen as she went in; a smaller version of Claribel, her fair hair thickly silvered but with a still pretty face.

Mother and daughter embraced happily and Claribel said: 'Oh, it's marvellous to be home again. What's for supper?'

'My potato soup, shepherd's pie and upside-down pineapple pudding.' She eyed her daughter. 'Been working hard, darling? We'll have a glass of sherry, shall we? Here's your father.'

Enoch and Toots were used to their weekend trips; they ate the food put ready for them and sat themselves down before the Aga while Rover settled close by and Claribel and her parents sat at the kitchen table drinking their sherry and catching up on the news.

'Sebastian has a new girlfriend,' said Mrs Brown. 'She's a nurse, not finished her training yet. He brought her down for the weekend—we like her, but of course he's young yet . . .'

'He's been qualified for a year, Mother.'

'Yes, dear, I know, but he seems so much younger than you.'

'Well, he is—three years, almost.'

There was a small silence. Claribel had had her share of young men but she had never been serious with any one of them; her mother, without saying a word, nevertheless allowed her anxiety to show. Her beautiful daughter was twenty-eight years old and it was inconceivable that she wouldn't marry. Each time Claribel went home, her mother contrived to bring the talk round to the young men she had met and always Claribel disappointed her.

To change the trend of her parent's obvious thoughts, Claribel said cheerfully, 'I almost missed the train. Luckily the orthopaedic man who is standing in for Mr Shutter happened to drive past and gave me a lift.'

'Nice?' asked her mother hopefully.

'No. Very terse and rude. He's Dutch.'

'What does he . . . Is he nice-looking?' asked Mrs Brown.

'Very. In an arrogant sort of way.'

'I don't see that his looks matter as long as he got Claribel to the station. Very civil of him,' observed her father.

He hadn't been civil, but Claribel let that pass. She finished her sherry and they went across the stone-flagged hallway to the dining-room, handsomely furnished in a shabby way with massive pieces inherited from her mother's family. The talk was all of local events while they ate and when they had washed up and had coffee, Claribel took herself off to bed; it had been a long day, rather more tiring than usual.

'I wonder what that Dutchman's like?' mused her mother over her knitting.

Mr Brown had a good book. 'I don't see that it matters; Claribel doesn't like him.'

Mrs Brown did a row in silence. 'We'll see,' she said. 'She hadn't a good word to say for him—a good sign.'

Her husband sighed. 'Mr dear, how you do run on. Besides, he's a consultant. Presumably hardly likely to take up with a physiotherapist.'

'Claribel is beautiful,' said her mother simply, as though that put an end to the argument.

The weekend went too fast; it always did. Claribel biked into Tisbury in the morning on various errands for her mother and to waste a good deal of time chatting with various friends she met there. In the afternoon she and her father took Rover for a walk along the bridle paths, which were short cuts leading to the villages around the little town. The weather had improved but it was wet underfoot. Claribel, in wellies, an old tweed skirt and an even older quilted jacket, had tied a scarf round her golden hair and borrowed her mother's woolly gloves. They got back for tea glowing with fresh air.

Sunday morning was taken up with church and leisurely chats after the service. Claribel had a lot of friends, most of them married now, and several with weddings in the offing. She was to be a bridesmaid at two of them and wandered off into the churchyard with the brides-to-be, to sit on a handy tombstone and discuss clothes.

The day wasn't too long enough. She collected Enoch and

Toots, packed her bag and in the early evening was driven
to Tisbury once more, very much inclined to agree with her
mother's remark that it was a pity that she couldn't stay at
home. But there was no hospital nearer than Salisbury and
no vacancies there. Besides, she had to stand on her own
two feet and make her own life. She might not marry; she
had had chances enough but none of them had been right
for her. She wasn't sure what kind of man she wanted for a
husband but she supposed that she would know when she
met him.

Meadow Road looked more dingy than ever as the taxi
drove down it, and her little semi-basement seemed
unbearably small and dark even with all the lights on. She
made tea, fed the cats and turned on the gas fire. She always
felt like this when she came back after a weekend at home;
in a day or two she would settle down.

She got out paper and envelopes, and wrote a stiff little
note to Mr van Borsele, enclosing a cheque for her railway
fare. In the morning she would take it to the lodge and ask a
porter to put it in the pigeonholes reserved for the
consultants and that would be the end of that.

She went to bed presently and fell asleep at once, to wake
in the night and wish that it wouldn't be the end; he was
such a thoroughly unpleasant man that it would be a
pleasure to reform him. She thought of several ways of
doing this before she slept again.

CHAPTER TWO

CLARIBEL was disappointed that she wouldn't be doing a ward round during the week; Mrs Green was back and there was a backlog of patients to deal with. The first few days of the week flew by and not once did she cast eyes on Mr van Borsele. She had handed in her note and the cheque and if she had expected an acknowledgment she was doomed to disappointment. Not that she had any wish to see him again, or so she told herself.

Not only was it a busy week, but the hospital was to hold its bi-annual bazaar at the weekend. It seemed a most unsuitable time for this, but since for very many years it had taken place on that particular Saturday, no one had considered changing it. Everyone was expected to help in some way. Minor royalty would be opening it, and the lecture hall would be turned into an indoor fair, the more expensive goods well to the forefront, the jumble and secondhand books at the back. Claribel was helping at the jumble stall; only the young and active were asked to do so for the local inhabitants relied upon it for a large proportion of their wardrobes and there was keen and sometimes ill-natured competition for clothes contributed by the patrons of the hospital.

The bazaar opened at two o'clock sharp and Miss Flute, marshalling her staff, reminded them to be there at one o'clock and not a minute later. Which meant that Saturday morning was rather a rush, what with having to shop for the weekend, clean the flat and do the washing. Claribel got into a needlecord skirt and a knitted jumper—the jumble stall caught all the icy draughts—tied her hair in a scarf, put on a quilted jacket, and went to catch her bus. It was a dreadful waste of a Saturday afternoon; she would have preferred to stay home with the cats, reading and making scones for tea.

The lecture hall was a hive of activity; she went straight to her stall and began to sort clothes into suitable piles. They wouldn't last long like that but the first bargain hunters would be able to snap up their choice without too much tossing of garments to and fro. There were two other girls on the stall, both good friends of hers, and, ready with ten minutes to spare, they had a pleasant gossip until a sudden subdued roar told them that the doors had been opened.

No one could buy anything until the bazaar had been officially opened. Minor royalty arrived exactly on time, made a brief speech, received the bouquet the hospital director's small daughter had been clutching, and declared the affair open, the signal for a concerted rush to the various stalls. Trade was brisk; the more élite toured the hall in the wake of royalty, buying beribboned coat hangers, lace pincushions and homemade jams, while the rest surged towards the jumble and secondhand books.

Claribel did a brisk trade; the mounds of clothing, hats and shoes disappeared rapidly. She knew a good many of her customers and wasn't surprised to see Mrs Snow edging her way along the stall, her arms already full of garments and a couple of hats.

'There you are, ducks,' said that lady cheerfully. 'Got a

nice haul here. 'Ere, I say, that nice young feller I told you about—'e's over there with the nobs.' She waved a cluttered hand towards the centre of the hall and Claribel perforce followed its direction. Sure enough, there was Mr van Borsele, head and shoulders above everyone else, talking to one of the hospital committee. He looked at her across the crowded hall and, although he gave no sign of having seen her, she turned her head at once. She took great care not to look around her again and indeed she had little time; by four o'clock she longed for a cup of tea but trade was too brisk for any of them to leave the stall. When the last customer had gone, an hour later, there was almost nothing to pack up and they made short work of it, grumbling among themselves in a good-natured way because their precious Saturday had been infringed upon. But as Miss Flute had told them, it had been well worth it; they had made a good deal of money and the hospital would be the richer by another kidney machine. They trooped off to wash their hands and do their faces and dispersed in a chorus of goodbyes. Miss Flute was standing by the door talking to Mr van Borsele as Claribel and several of the other girls reached it. She stretched out a hand as Claribel went by so that she had to stop.

'Claribel, Mr van Borsele has kindly offered to give me a lift home; he will have to go past Meadow Road and says it's no trouble to drop you off.'

Claribel said quickly, 'Oh, please don't bother—there will be plenty of buses.'

'No bother,' said Mr van Borsele smoothly. 'Shall we go? I'm sure you must both want your tea.'

She found herself sitting behind him, watching Miss Flute chatting away with surprising animation. They were on the best of terms, she reflected peevishly, and only occasionally did Miss Flute address some remark to her over a shoulder.

Miss Flute lived alone in a tiny mews flat behind Charing Cross station and Mr van Borsele got out and opened the door for her and saw her safely inside before coming back to his car.

He opened the door and studied Claribel. 'Come in front?' he enquired so pleasantly that she had no choice but to get out and get in again beside him. He shut the door on her with the air of a man who had got his way, got in beside her and drove back along the Embankment, over Waterloo Bridge and into Stamford Street. It had turned into a dull afternoon and Meadow Road, when they reached it, looked drab. He stopped outside her flat and turned to look at her.

'Are you going to invite me in for tea?'

It was the last thing she had expected. 'Well, I hadn't intended to but if you'd like to come in, do.' That sounded rude; she amended it hastily, 'What I mean is, I didn't imagine you would want to come to tea.'

He said gravely. 'You shouldn't let your imagination run away with you, Claribel—and I should like to come to tea. That was an infernal afternoon.'

She laughed then, quite forgetting that she didn't like him. 'Yes, it always is, but it's only twice a year. Such a pity it has to be on a Saturday, though.'

They got out of the car and he opened the door and stood aside for her to go in. The cats rushed to meet them and he bent to tickle their heads and then stood up; his size made the room even smaller. She said, 'Do take off your coat—there's a hook in the lobby. I'll put the kettle on.'

She threw her coat on the bed and changed her shoes,

decided her face and hair would have to do and went into the tiny kitchen. There was a cake she had baked that morning and one of her mother's homemade loaves. She sliced and buttered, cut the cake, added a cup and saucer to the tray and made the tea.

Mr van Borsele was sitting in the largest of the chairs with a cat on either side of him. He got up as she opened the door, took the tray from her and set it on the small table on one side of the fireplace and went to fetch the cake. The cats followed him in what she considered to be a slavish fashion and when he sat down again, resumed their places on either side of him.

'You like cats?' Hardly a conversational gambit, but they would have to talk about something.

'Yes. My grandmother has two—Burmese.' He accepted his tea and sat back comfortably and she found herself wondering what his grandmother was like—somehow he was such a self-contained man, obviously used to getting his own way, that it was hard to imagine her—a small, doting mouse of a woman, perhaps? And his wife? If he was married.

He was watching her, his dark eyes amused. 'I have two of my own,' he told her. 'Common or garden cats with no pedigrees, and two equally well-bred dogs who keep them in order.'

She passed him the bread and butter. 'And your wife? She likes animals?'

The amusement deepened but he answered gravely, 'I am not yet married.' He took a bite. 'Homemade bread. Are you a cook, Claribel?'

'Well, I can, you know, but my mother is quite super.'

She watched him consume several slices and made polite

conversation. She didn't like him, she reminded herself, but there was something rather pathetic about a very large man eating his tea with such enjoyment. As she offered him the cake, she wondered briefly where he was living while he was in London.

'Do you go home frequently?' He sounded casually polite and she found herself talking about Tisbury and her friends there and how she loved her weekends. He led her on gently so that she told him a good deal more than she realised; she was telling him about Sebastian and how clever he was when the phone rang.

She was going out that evening—one of the girls she worked with was getting engaged and there was to be a party; she wanted to make sure that Claribel would be there.

'Yes, of course. I haven't forgotten. Eight o'clock. I'll be ready at half past seven.'

'I'm so happy,' burbled the voice at the other end.

'Well, of course you are.' Claribel smiled at the phone as she put down the receiver.

Mr van Borsele was watching her with an expressionless face.

As she sat down again he said easily, 'A date this evening? I'll be on my way. A pleasant hour, Claribel, between this afternoon's tedium and the evening's pleasure.' He added thoughtfully, 'Surprising, really, for you still aren't sure if you like me, are you?'

He stood up and she got to her feet, facing him. She gave him a clear look from her beautiful eyes. 'No, I'm not sure, but it doesn't really matter, does it? There must be any number of women who—who admire you!'

'Probably.' He spoke without conceit. 'But I'm really

only concerned with one girl, not untold numbers.'

'Oh, well in that case it doesn't matter what I think about you, does it, Mr van Borsele?'

He shrugged into his coat, offered a gentle hand to Enoch and Toots and went to the door. He didn't answer her, only wished her the politest of goodnights as he left.

Several times during the evening she found herself wishing that Mr van Borsele had been there, which, considering she didn't like him, seemed strange.

Back in her flat, lying in bed with the cats curled up at her feet, she decided it was because he was so much older than the young men who had been at the party, mostly newly qualified housemen or final-year students. 'After all, I am getting a bit long in the tooth,' muttered Claribel to her unresponsive companions.

Of course she knew other older men. There was one in particular, Frederick Frost, the junior registrar on the orthopaedic wards, a serious man who had given her to understand that he had singled her out for his attention. She had gone out with him on several occasions now, and liked him well enough although she found him singularly lacking in romantic feeling. He would be a splendid husband; he would also be very dull.

Sometimes she lay in bed and wondered if she had been wise to refuse the offers of several young men who had wished to marry her. She hadn't loved any of them; liked them well enough, even been fond of them, but that was all. Somewhere in the world, she was convinced, was the man she could love for always; she had no idea what he would look like but she supposed that when she met him she would know that he was the one. Only here she was, the wrong end of the twenties, and it looked as though she would never meet him.

Frederick had asked her to spend Sunday afternoon with him; she came back from church in the morning, ate her solitary lunch and took a bus to Hyde Park where they were to meet. Frederick believed in good fresh air and exercise; he walked her briskly from the Marble Arch entrance to Green Park and thence to St James's Park, talking rather prosily all the way. Claribel, brought up in the country and fond of walking, nonetheless was relieved when they finally reached the Mall and Trafalgar Square and entered a modest café for tea and toasted teacakes.

Frederick was on duty at the hospital at six o'clock. He saw her on to a bus, assuring her that she looked all the better for the exercise they had taken that afternoon, and invited her to repeat it on the following Sunday.

Claribel's feet ached and her head buzzed with the various diagnoses he had been entertaining with her; she said hastily that she would be going home, thanked him prettily for her tea and sank thankfully on to a seat in the bus.

The cats were pleased to see her and her little room looked cosy as she went indoors. She kicked off her shoes, took off her outdoor things and turned on the gas fire. She would sit and read for an hour before getting her supper.

It was barely ten minutes before the knocker on her front door was given a sound thump. She got up reluctantly, dislodging the cats, and went to open the door.

Mr van Borsele loomed over her. 'I thought I told you never to answer the door without making sure that you knew the caller,' he said testily. 'Well, won't you ask me in?'

'Why should I?' she snapped. 'Banging on my door . . . Next time I shan't open it.'

'What makes you think there will be a next time?' he asked smoothly.

Only by a great effort did she stop herself from grinding her teeth. 'There won't be if I can help it,' she assured him coldly.

'Having cleared up that knotty point, may I come in? There's something I wish to discuss with you.'

'Could it not wait until Monday?' She added crossly, 'It's Sunday, you know.'

'Monday will be too late.' He suddenly smiled at her with great charm. 'If I might come in?'

She stood back reluctantly and remembered that she wasn't wearing her shoes. At the same time Mr van Borsele observed, 'Been walking? Don't bother to put your shoes on for me.' He studied her stockinged feet. 'You have nice ankles.'

He was impossible! She said stonily, 'You wished to say something urgently, Mr van Borsele?'

'Ah, yes. There is an orthopaedic clinic in Whitechapel; it seems there is a flu bug there which has laid low the visiting consultant and three of the physiotherapists. They have asked us for help, and Miss Flute suggested you might accompany me—she can get a part-time girl in to do your work at our clinic for the morning, and I happen to be free until the afternoon. The clinic starts at eight o'clock and lasts until about noon.'

'Why me?' asked Claribel.

'You seem to be a sensible young woman, able to cope.'

'Am I given any choice?'

'Not really. It's a busy clinic; takes fringe cases from several hospitals; I believe the patients come quite long distances.'

Claribel eyed him carefully; he didn't appear to be anything else but serious but one couldn't tell. She said slowly, 'Very well, Mr van Borsele.'

'Splendid. One does appreciate a willing volunteer.' His voice was all silk so that she darted a suspicious look at him. He met her eye with a look of bland innocence and she was sure that he was finding something very amusing behind it.

'I am not a willing volunteer,' she protested. 'You yourself have just said . . .'

He interrupted her in a soothing voice, 'No, no, of course you're not; merely doing your duty, however irksome. I will call for you at seven o'clock precisely; that will give us time to find our way around.'

He had been standing all this time and so had she. 'You have had a pleasant afternoon? A few hours in the country, perhaps?'

She thought of her aching feet. 'Hyde Park and Green Park and St James's Park.'

'Delightful in pleasant company.'

She thought of Frederick. 'I dare say,' she sighed.

'Never alone, Claribel?'

'No,' she added, forgetting to whom she was talking. 'I would have liked to be at home.' She looked up at him with her lovely eyes and was startled at the look on his face, gone so quickly that she supposed that she had imagined it.

He said casually, 'One can be lonely even with companions. Do you suppose we might dine together this evening? I had to cancel a date so that I could get arrangements made for the morning and I'm sure we could remain polite towards each other for a couple of hours; we don't need to talk unless you want to.'

While he spoke he contrived to look lonely and hungry

and in need of companionship; Claribel was aware that he was doing it deliberately, but all the same it would be heartless to refuse. Besides, there was only cold ham in the fridge . . . She said quickly before she thought better of it, 'Very well, Mr van Borsele, I'll dine with you, but I have to see to Enoch and Toots first.' She remembered her manners. 'Do sit down, I'll only be ten minutes.' At the door she paused. 'Nowhere posh—I'm not dressed to go out.'

He cast an eye over her person. 'You will do very well as you are. Only put your shoes on.'

He took her to Chelsea, to a restaurant just off the Kings Road: English Garden, quite small but pleasantly surrounded by a conservatory full of greenery and flowers. They ate traditional English food, beautifully cooked and served, and rather to Claribel's surprise she found herself enjoying not only the food but her companion's conversation. Not that she discovered anything much about him from his talk; he talked about Holland, touched lightly on his work, went on to discuss several West End plays he had been to and then led her on, ever so gently, to talk about herself. It was only later that she realised this, annoyed with herself for telling him so much, especially as she hadn't found out anything at all about him. She had asked, in a roundabout way, how long he would be in London, but somehow he hadn't answered her. Lying in her bed, thinking about it, she promised herself that she would have another go in the morning.

Perhaps he wasn't as bad as she had first thought, she decided sleepily; he had driven her back to her flat, opened her door for her and then bidden her a cheerful goodnight. She had been debating whether to ask him in for a final cup of coffee as they drove, but the very briskness of his manner decided her against it.

She was ready and waiting for him when he arrived the next morning. They exchanged good mornings but, beyond a few civil remarks about the weather, which for early April was chilly and damp, they had nothing to say to each other, and once at the clinic they each went their own way, to meet again presently on a strictly professional basis.

Even if they had felt inclined, there was no opportunity to talk. The clinic bulged with patients of all sorts, a good-natured crowd with its crutches and slings and neck braces, sitting patiently and rather noisily in the waiting-room. There were two physiotherapists there besides Claribel. They shared out the work between them and long after Mr van Borsele had seen his last patient, they were all hard at it. It was after one o'clock when they began to clear up and tidy away the apparatus.

He'll be gone, reflected Claribel as she got out of her overall. I'll have to get a bus—it'll take hours. She dragged a comb through her hair, dabbed powder on to her nose and got into her coat. The other two girls were waiting to leave. She said goodbye and went out through the side door and saw the Rolls parked in front of it. Mr van Borsele was at the wheel, looking impassive. He got out and opened the door, and ushered her in without a word.

'There was no need to wait,' protested Claribel, faintly peevish, and was taken aback when he replied,

'Well, of course there wasn't, only I chose to do so.'

'Well, really . . .'

'I have found,' remarked Mr van Borsele blandly as he sent the car smoothly to join the traffic, 'that the English language is littered with useless phrases.' And, while she was getting over that, 'Unfortunately there is not sufficient time to have lunch, but one of the registrars assures me that Nick's Diner, just round the corner from Jerome's can offer a sound beef sandwich and good coffee. We will go there.'

He had no more to say and for the life of her Claribel could think of no conversation suitable for the occasion. She knew very well that if she raised any objections she would be either ignored or talked out of it; she held her tongue.

The streets were comparatively empty; she got out, still wordless, when Mr van Borsele parked tidily in the consultant's car park and walked beside him as he strode out of the hospital forecourt into the dingy street beyond. Nick's Diner was down a side street, one side of which was taken up by St Jerome's looming walls. It was small and rather dark and the plastic tables were crowded close together, but it was clean and the aroma from the coffee machine caused Claribel to wrinkle her pretty nose.

The little place was full but as they went in two medical students got up from a table near the door. 'Over here, sir,' they chorused and ushered Claribel into a chair, accepting his thanks with a kind of reverence which made her smile a little, and rushed out. Probably they had skipped a lecture.

The proprietor, a small wizened man who had been there so long no one could remember when he first appeared, joined them at once, gave the table a wipe and bent a differential ear to Mr van Borsele's request for beef sandwiches and coffee.

'Couldn't 'ave chosen better,' he assured them. 'Nice bit o' beef I've got—cuts like silk—and good 'olesome bread to go with it, too; none of that white flannel stuff from a factory. Be with you in a couple of shakes, sir.'

Sir sat back and looked around him and then across the

little table at Claribel. 'Hardly a place I would like to bring anyone. You're not feeling insulted or having injured feelings, I hope?'

'Me? Heavens, no.' She added waspishly, 'I'm not a snob.'

'I hardly imagined that you were. Nor am I, although I can see that you think that I am. But one would normally choose a rather more fitting background for a girl as pretty as you are, Claribel.'

He watched her blush.

'Why are you called Claribel?'

'My mother liked—still likes—historical romances. Just before I was born she was reading a tale where the heroine was called Claribel—so I was christened that. She rather wanted Mariabella, which is another version of it, but Father put his foot down.'

'And your brother?' The question was put casually.

'Sebastian? Oh, Mother was into Shakespeare in a big way.' She bit into a sandwich. 'Why were . . .' she began, but stopped just in time and took another bite; she must remember that he was a consultant and, from what Miss Flute had let drop, an important one in his own field.

'My name, as you know, is Marc, spelled with a C, and, since the conversation tends to be rather more personal than usual, I am thirty-six years old. At the moment I am not prepared to divulge more details of my life.'

She choked on some of the wholesome bread. 'I am not in the least interested in you, Mr van Borsele.' She spoke with a cold dignity marred by having a mouthful of sandwich.

He laughed. 'What a touchy girl you are! How old are you, Claribel?'

She said indignantly, 'Don't you know that you never ask

any girl how old she is?'

'Yes, I know, but you aren't any girl, Claribel. You look about eighteen, but of course, you're not.' He waited for her to reply, his eyebrows raised.

He was utterly impossible and getting worse all the time; she couldn't imagine Frederick saying a thing like that. Come to think of it, she couldn't imagine Frederick . . . He had become so vague she could barely remember what he looked like. 'I'm twenty-eight.' She added coldly, 'Is there anything else you want to know?'

'Oh, a great deal, but unfortunately we are pressed for time.'

She put down her empty coffee cup. 'I really have to go. Thank you for my lunch, Mr van Borsele.'

He got up with her, paid the bill, and followed her into the street. 'What's his name, this young man who walks you through London parks until your feet ache?'

She said quickly, 'Oh, you wouldn't know him.' She spoke so hurriedly and loudly that he had his answer and smiled to himself. 'I'm not being nosey, just making polite conversation,' he assured her blandly. 'Are you—what is the term?—going steady with him?'

They were crossing the forecourt and in a few moments she would be able to escape his endless questions. 'No, of course not.' She was an honest girl, so she added, 'Well, I suppose I could if I wanted to, only I don't. It's just that he wants someone to go for a walk with.'

Mr van Borsele gave a chortle of laughter and she said crossly, 'Don't you dare laugh.'

'No, no, my dear girl, I'm laughing for all the wrong reasons. You have too kind a heart; I suspect you don't discourage this young man with no name. I suspect also that you get dates enough and can pick and choose.'

She said seriously, 'Well, yes, I suppose so, but I'm not very, well—modern.' She stared up at him with a grave face. 'You won't know what I mean.'

'On the contrary, I know very well.' He smiled suddenly and she discovered that he was a kind man after all. 'If ever I should invite you out again, Claribel, it will be on the strict understanding that you have no need to be modern. Being well past my first youth, I'm not modern, either.'

They had reached the side door leading to the physiotherapy department. He opened it for them and with a brief nod walked away.

She scuttled down the covered way, already late. Perhaps she liked him after all, she thought confusedly; well, some of the time at any rate.

Miss Flute was surprisingly mild about her lateness; someone had covered for her and Mrs Green had gone to the wards. 'Mr van Borsele had a round on Women's Ward,' she observed. 'I didn't dare wait for you for I wasn't sure how long you would be. Were you very busy?'

Claribel, tearing into her overall, told her.

'You've had no lunch?' asked Miss Flute worriedly.

Claribel went faintly pink. 'Well, Mr van Borsele gave me a lift back and I—we had a sandwich in Nick's Diner.'

'Very civil of him,' answered Miss Flute briskly. 'There's that nervous old lady with the hip—will you take her on? She's so scared, she needs someone gentle and unhurried.'

'Unhurried?' Claribel cast her eyes to the ceiling. 'Miss Flute, I'll be lucky to get away by six o'clock.'

'Well, you've had a nice morning, haven't you, dear?' suggested Miss Flute and went back into her office.

Claribel, pacifying her elderly patient, decided that, yes, she had had a nice morning. It was a pity that she had been too late to go to the ward for Mr van Borsele's round; perhaps Miss Flute would send her to Men's Orthopaedic for the next consultant's round; she had been treating several patients there.

But Miss Flute, it seemed, had other ideas. Claribel spent the next two days in Out-Patients with the senior registrar and Frederick and didn't so much as catch a glimpse of Mr van Borsele. Life was really rather dull, she reflected, getting her supper while Toots and Enoch sat and watched her; it might be a good idea if she were to go home at the weekend. 'It would be a nice change for all of us,' she assured the cats as she sat down to her solitary meal.

She bumped into him—literally—as she crossed the courtyard to go home on the following day. He put out a had to steady her and said without preamble, 'I'm going to Bath for the weekend. I'll drop you off at Tisbury and pick you up on the way back.'

'Oh, but I . . .' She caught his eye and stopped then began again, 'I really hadn't intended . . .' Under that dark gaze she faltered again. She said slowly, because she felt compelled to, 'I should like that very much, Mr van Borsele.' She added hastily, 'To go home, I mean.' She wondered why he grinned suddenly. 'Shall I meet you here, and at what time?'

'Haven't you forgotten your cats? I'll pick you up—half past six at your flat, and mind you are ready.'

He nodded his goodbye and had gone before she could frame so much as a single word.

She told Enoch and Toots when she got home and, mindful that she might get away late on Friday afternoon, put her overnight things in a bag and decided what she would wear; before she went to work in the morning she would put her clothes ready. Mr van Borsele might have offered her a lift, but he was quite capable of going without her if she kept him waiting for more than a minute or so.

Friday's clinic was overflowing and, to make matters worse, Mrs Green went home during the morning, feeling, as she put it, not at all the thing. That meant Claribel would have to take on several more patients as well as her own, for two of the other girls were at the ante-natal clinic and the other two were only just qualified and needed an eye kept upon them.

Claribel got home half an hour late. To have sat down, kicked off her shoes and drunk the teapot dry would have been bliss; as it was, she fed the cats, showered, changed into a short jacket and plaid pleated skirt, got her aching feet into her rather smart boots, popped the cats into their basket and opened the door to Mr van Borsele, looking as composed as if she had spent the entire day doing nothing much.

He ran a knowledgeable eye over her person. 'Tired? You can doze in the car.'

A remark which incensed her after her efforts. But she hadn't noticed the shadows under her eyes or the lack of colour in her cheeks.

She wished him a good evening, adding that she had no desire to doze. 'Besides, you might want me to map-read for you.'

He took her bag from her and stowed it in the boot and then put the cat basket on the back seat. 'Straight down the A303, once I'm on it. You can wake up when we're nearby and tell me where to go from there.'

She said huffily, 'Well, if you want me to sleep all the way I'll do my best. There's no need for you to talk.'

He shut the door and made sure that it was locked. 'In you get,' he urged her. 'You're a bit edgy but I dare say you've had a hard day with Mrs Green away.' He got in beside her and turned to look at her. 'You thought that I wouldn't wait if you weren't ready? I am an impatient man, Claribel, but for some things I am prepared to wait—if necessary, for ever.'

She puzzled over this and found no clear answer. 'Have you had a busy day?' she asked politely.

'Very. A quiet weekend will be delightful. You know Bath?'

'Quite well—we go there to shop sometimes. You—you said you had friends there?'

He was driving west out of London in heavy traffic. 'Yes, they live at Limpley Stoke—not friends; my young sister and her husband.'

'Oh, she's Dutch, too . . .' It was a silly remark and she waited for him to say so. But he didn't.

'She spent some years over here at boarding school. She's happy here and of course they go to Holland frequently.'

Claribel tried to imagine his sister. Tall, short; thin, fat?

'She's not in the least like me: small, fair and very slim.' He glanced sideways at her. 'Close your eyes, Claribel, you are tired.'

She frowned. Tired so often meant plain. The thought didn't stop her doing as she was told; she was asleep within minutes.

CHAPTER THREE

THEY were racing past Stonehenge when she awoke, feeling much refreshed.

'Feel better?' asked Mr van Borsele.

'Yes, thank you. There's a turning on the left once you've got to Wylye; it's a side road to Tisbury. You can get back on to the A303 if you go through Hindon. If you go via Warminster it's the quickest way to Bath.'

'Oh, dear, oh, dear. You can't get rid of me quickly enough, can you, Claribel?'

Any sleepiness she might have felt evaporated in a trice. 'I am merely trying to be helpful; you're coming out of your way to take me home and I am grateful but I don't wish to impose upon you.'

'Very commendable, Claribel, your thoughtfulness does you credit.' She could hear the laugh in his voice. 'Let me hasten to assure you that on one has, or ever will, impose upon me. I do what I like and I contrive to get my own way.'

'How very arrogant. I am surprised that you have any friends, Mr van Borsele.'

'Ah, but I am also cunning; I hide my arrogance under a smooth exterior.' He contrived to sound ill-done-by. 'I am in fact both soft-hearted and lovable when you get to know me.'

Claribel felt laughter bubbling up inside her. She gave a

little chuckle. 'What a good thing that we're almost there or I might begin to feel sorry for you. The gate is on the left; it's just a short drive to the house.'

Light shone through the downstairs windows and as he drove slowly up to the door Mrs Brown flung it open. She hadn't got her spectacles on, so she blinked short-sightedly as the car stopped. 'Darling, you got a lift? How nice—bring them in, whoever it is.' She came a little nearer and saw Mr van Borsele move from the car. 'My goodness!' she observed cheerfully. 'What a large man, and isn't that a Rolls-Royce?'

Claribel skipped round the car and embraced her parent. 'Mother, this is Mr van Borsele from the hospital. He kindly gave me a lift home—he's going to Bath.'

She tucked an arm through her mother's. 'My mother, Mr van Borsele.'

He shook hands gently, smiling down at her. 'How do you do, Mrs Brown?'

'Come inside,' invited Mrs Brown, beaming up at him. Have a cup of coffee—something to eat? Sandwiches?'

'You're very kind, but I am expected at Bath this evening.'

'My husband would like to meet you. Are you taking Claribel back?'

He glanced at Claribel, standing silently. 'Sunday evening, about six o'clock? Perhaps I shall have the pleasure of meeting Mr Brown then.'

'That will be delightful. Supper?'

He shook his head and if he didn't feel regret he was pretending very well indeed. 'I've a late evening date—I must be back in town by nine o'clock at the latest.'

He shook hands again, gave Claribel the briefest of smiles

and got back into his car.

They watched him drive away and Mrs Brown said, 'What a very nice man. Is he a friend, darling?'

'No, Mother, he's not. We argue whenever we meet, which is seldom. He has a nasty caustic tongue.'

'Most unpleasant.' They were inside the house, the door shut. 'His patients must detest him?'

Claribel had been brought up to be fair and not to fib unless she really had to. 'Well, as a matter of fact, they all dote on him; he's quite different with his patients.'

She had tossed her jacket on to a chair and they had gone into the sitting-room. Mrs Brown shot a quick look at her. 'So he must be nice. It was kind of him to bring you home, darling. A pity he didn't stay for a cup of coffee.'

Claribel shook up a cushion and let Toots and Enoch out of their basket. 'Yes, I suppose I should have suggested it.'

Her mother went to the door. 'Well, he's coming on Sunday. Supper is ready, darling, and there's plenty for you—your father won't be back just yet. He's over at Bradshaw's Farm advising them about selling the ten-acre field. It's a lovely surprise having you back for the weekend.'

Her father came in just as they were sitting down in the panelled dining-room across the hall. He helped her to a portion of one of Mrs Brown's excellent steak and kidney pies with the observation that it was a treat to see her and how had she got home, anyway?

'One of the orthopaedic consultants was going to Bath for the weekend; he offered me a lift. He'll pick me up on Sunday evening, Father.'

'One of your beaux?' Mr Brown wanted to know. It was a long-standing joke in the family that she was choosy and would end up an old maid. No one believed it, but just lately Claribel had had moments of anxiety that the right man wasn't going to turn up and the joke wouldn't be a joke any longer.

She laughed because he expected that she would. 'Oh, not likely, Father,' she said brightly. 'He's a consultant; they live on a higher plane than any one else. Besides, we don't get on very well.'

'No? The more decent of him to give you a lift. I look forward to meeting him.'

She consoled herself with the thought that the meeting would be brief. She even forgot Mr van Borsele for quite long periods at the weekend—there seemed so much to occupy her: gardening, driving her mother into Salisbury to shop on Saturday morning, taking the dog for a walk, and going back to the vicarage after church on Sunday because the vicar's eldest son was home on leave from some far-flung spot. They had grown up together, more or less, and she thought of him as another brother; it was mid-afternoon before he walked her back to her home and, naturally enough, stayed for tea. Claribel just had time to fling her things into her bag and make sure that the cats were safely in the kitchen ready to be scooped into their basket before Mr van Borsele arrived.

She had expected that he would spend an obligatory five minutes talking polite nothings to her father and mother, settle her and the cats in the car with dispatch, and drive away to his evening date. She might have known it; he was a man who did what he liked when he liked, and it seemed that he liked to stay an hour, drinking her mother's excellent coffee and discussing international law with her father. She sat quietly, handing coffee cups when called upon, feeling vaguely sorry for whoever it was he was taking out that evening. A girl, of course; and if I were that girl, reflected Claribel, I wouldn't go out with him; I'd have a headache or go to bed or something—or find someone else to have supper with.

She glanced up and found his dark eyes resting thoughtfully on her so that she felt as guilty as though she had spoken her thoughts out loud. He smiled suddenly and she smiled back before she could stop herself.

He got to his feet. 'We should be going.' He made his goodbyes with a grave courtesy which she could see impressed her parents and then ushered her out to the car. Toots and Enoch were handed in, final goodbyes were said and he drove away.

'You're going to be late for your evening out,' said Claribel as they left Tisbury behind.

'I think not. It's half past seven; we can be back soon after nine o'clock; my date is for ten o'clock. The road should be pretty clear at this time of the evening.' He added, 'I imagine you don't want to be too late back.'

The roads were almost empty; it was a wet evening and until they reached the outskirts of London there was nothing to hinder them. Claribel, who had allowed herself to wonder if they might stop for coffee, realised that her companion had no such intention. She was deposited inside her front door with the cats and her bag very shortly before half past nine, bidden a casual goodnight and had her politely phrased thanks dismissed just as casually. He had had little to say during the drive, and that of a general nature; she was left with the strong impression that, having done his duty, he was only too glad to be shot of her. She wished him a pleasant evening in a voice which belied her words and closed the door on his departing back.

'And that's the last time,' declared Claribel, not quite clear what she meant.

She woke to a lovely morning: sunshine and blue skies and a breathy little wind with warmth in it. It being April, it was liable to rain before she got home, but that didn't stop her from wearing a knitted suit with a matching blouse. It was in chestnut brown which went very nicely with her pale hair and, since it was a Monday morning and her spirits needed a boost she wore a pair of high-heeled shoes, deceptively simple and, for that reason, expensive. She left for work feeling pleased with her appearance and attracted several wolf whistles as she went to catch her bus. Vulgar, but good for a girl's esteem.

Mr van Borsele, passing her in the hospital forecourt, didn't whistle, although he slowed the car as he went past her and took a good look. She gave him a pleasant smile and walked on, feeling a deep satisfaction, although she wasn't sure why.

It was several days before she saw him again. Miss Flute had kept her in the department, dealing with the regular patients, most of whom came at least once a week, and often twice. They were all hard work, some harder than others, and she was glad to get back to her little flat in the evening and cook her supper and go to bed early. Frederick had wanted her to go with him to a concert and one of the housemen had suggested that they might go to a disco, but she found herself singularly lacking in enthusiasm for either suggestion.

All the more surprising then that when Mr van Borsele, towards the end of the week, thumped on her door, she should admit him with something like pleased anticipation.

And not without reason; he had tickets for *The Phantom of the Opera*, and took it for granted that she would go with him.

'Why me?' she asked.

He sat himself down in the easiest chair and the cats got onto his knee.

'I suppose that you have had a busy day—so have I. I don't want to make small talk and I don't think you would want that either. On the other hand I don't want to go alone.'

'How charmingly put,' said Claribel, her breast heaving with indignation. 'Just the sort of invitation any woman would jump at. No, I won't come.'

'Supper afterwards?' coaxed Mr van Borsele in his most beguiling voice. 'I believe the music is a delight, just right after a tiresome day. Was your day tiresome, Claribel?'

'Yes, very. And I'm tired; I was just going to get my supper.'

'Make coffee instead, jump into something pretty and we'll be off. We have an hour.'

She had wanted to see *The Phantom of the Opera*, but Frederick wasn't the man to waste his money on anything so frivolous as the theatre, certainly not a man to bang on the door and take it for granted that she would go anyway. She said, 'There isn't enough time—I haven't fed Enoch and Toots.'

He heaved himself out of the chair. 'Go and dress; I'll see to the coffee and the cats.' He wandered off into the kitchen and she went to her bedroom and poked about in her wardrobe. Only when she had showered and changed into a pretty patterned dress did she remember that she hadn't said she would go with him. Impulsively she padded into the sitting-room with her shoes in her hand. 'I haven't said I'll go . . .' she began.

'Well, you can't sit around all evening in that dress. I've fed the cats and the coffee is ready. What a pretty dress, and I like your hair.'

She stared at him. 'But I haven't done it yet.' It was hanging down her back, a golden damp tangle. She had forgotten it when she had gone into the sitting-room; now she felt very self-conscious about it. 'If you wouldn't mind pouring the coffee I'll only be a few minutes.'

She did her face rapidly, swept her hair tidily into a chignon and went back to join him. He was standing by the window, a mug in his hand; he handed her hers and told her to drink up and not waste any more time.

She took a heartening sip. 'What a most unfair thing to say,' she pointed out. 'I had no intention of going out and I'm only coming with you because . . . well, because . . .'

'You want to?' He smiled at her and she gulped her coffee and burnt her tongue.

The show was marvellous; Claribel sat spellbound, her eyes on the stage listening and watching, afraid to miss a single moment of it. Mr van Borsele sat back in his seat, watching her. During the interval he took her to the foyer for a drink and listened to her rather breathless remarks about the show, agreeing gravely, the perfect companion. When the curtain came down for the very last time, he led her out to the car and drove to the Savoy Grill and gave her a delicious supper: lobster thermidor, with a mouth-watering salad, *chaudfroid* of raspberries and endless coffee and petits fours.

'Working tomorrow?' he enquired casually.

'Yes. There's an ante-natal clinic in the morning and Out-patients' Department in the afternoon. The orthopaedic registrar takes it, but you know that, of course.'

She nibbled a petit four. 'When does Mr Shutter come back?'

'Next week.'

She waited for him to say more but he remained utterly silent. Presently she asked, 'Do you leave then?'

'Within a day or two of his return, yes. Will you miss me?'

'Mrs Green has been working with you . . .'

'I asked if you would miss me, Claribel.'

For something to do she poured more coffee. 'Well, yes, I think I shall.'

'You will doubtless have as many dates as you can cope with?'

'Yes.' She was quite serious. 'But they're not like you.'

'God forbid! Tell me, Claribel, what do you intend to do with your life?'

The wine she had drunk at supper had loosened her tongue. 'I like my work—it's very rewarding, you know—but I'd like to get married and have children, only I'm getting a bit . . .'

'But you must have had offers of marriage?'

'Several, only they've never been . . . I'm not sure . . . How will I know when I meet the right man, if I ever do? And perhaps it's too late.'

'You'll know, and it's never too late. But most of us make do with what we get offered and make a success of it, too.'

'You mean we don't always meet the right person?'

'I don't mean that at all; almost all of us do, but we don't always realise it.'

'Oh.' She thought about that. 'Don't you think that

people should marry because they fall in love?'

'Well, of course I do, but there are a dozen other excellent reasons for marrying and none of them have anything to do with falling in love. And they make for sound marriages, too.'

She eyed him across the table, faintly muzzy from the wine. 'Are you going to get married, Mr van Borsele?' A question she wouldn't have dreamed of asking, only the wine was talking now.

He smiled a little, 'Yes, Claribel, I have the urge to settle down and become a family man.'

'In Holland, of course?'

'Of course.'

'I hope you will be very happy.' The wine had taken over with a vengeance. 'She'll be small and dainty and agree with everything you do and say and she'll do exactly as you wish. I can't imagine you marrying anyone else.'

'You're letting your imagination run away with you, dear girl.' He gave her a mocking smile which acted like a shower of cold water, drowning the rest of the wine.

She muttered, 'I'm sure you will be very happy, Mr van Borsele.'

'I'm sure I shall be, too.'

She was very conscious of having been rude. 'I'm sorry I said that,' she told him. 'I didn't mean a word of it. Do you mind if we go now? It's quite late . . .'

He asked for the bill and his smile wasn't mocking any more. 'You have no need to apologise, although I don't think I shall take your advice.'

He talked of everyday things as they drove back, and having seen her safely indoors, bade her a cheerful farewell and goodnight and got back into his car, barely giving her time to thank him for the evening.

She didn't see him the next day, but she hadn't expected to. The following Tuesday she spent the day in Intensive Care, helping one of the patients to adjust to breathing normally again. It was on Wednesday in the clinic at the end of a busy morning, with only Mrs Snow between her and a brief lunch, that that lady came trotting in.

'There you are, dearie,' she began as she started to peel off a variety of woollen garments. 'Wot a week I've had—there's me youngest out of work again and the old man with toothache and me 'aving to look after young Claude while 'is mum goes to the ante-natal . . .'

Claribel arranged her on a stool by a low table, put a cushion under her arm and ran a gentle hand over it. 'Been doing your exercises?' she wanted to know.

'Well, now, love, I 'aven't 'ad much time, wot with the ironing and that.'

Claribel was massaging gently. 'No, I don't suppose you do have much time,' she agreed. 'Could you manage to do a few exercises before you get up? Just lifting your arm like I showed you and swinging it a bit?'

'Anything to please yer, ducks. Where were you last week? I 'ad a cross old dragon, got real narked 'cause I couldn't touch me 'ead.'

'I had to go to an outside clinic—they were short of staff.'

'All on yer own?'

'Oh, my, no, there were other staff there.'

'That nice young man I saw—'e's gone back to Holland. Ain't it a shame? I rather fancied him. I just 'appened to be passing as 'e was shaking 'ands with Mr Shutter and I 'eard him say, "Well, I'll be off—I plan to catch the evening ferry from Harwich." She breathed a gusty sign, redolent of onion, all over Claribel. 'Silly ter say I'll miss 'im,' she observed and Claribel, rather to her surprise, agreed with her silently. So silly really; she hardly knew him and she still wasn't quite sure if she liked him, but here she was regretting his departure. And without so much as wishing her goodbye. He could at least have mentioned it when he had brought her home from the play; he had said within a day or two of Mr Shutter's return and Mr Shutter had returned only that morning . . .

'Tired, ducks?' asked Mrs Snow kindly. 'All that rubbing you do . . . I can come next week; perhaps you'll be feeling more the thing.'

'I never felt better, Mrs Snow.' Claribel resumed her massage and the soothing chat with it.

As they ate their sandwiches together she said to Miss Flute, 'Mr van Borsele didn't waste much time in going back to Holland. Perhaps he didn't like it here.'

Miss Flute bit daintily into a sausage roll. 'Didn't you see him? He came in to say goodbye. Said he'd enjoyed every minute of being here; hoped to come back some day. He and Mr Shutter were students together, you know.'

Claribel said lightly, 'Oh, were they?' It seemed that Miss Flute knew more about him than she herself did. But then, why should he have told her anything about himself?

She felt cross for the rest of the day and when Frederick met her on her way out of the hospital and asked her to go to a concert with him on the Sunday evening, she agreed, instantly regretting it. Frederick no longer interested her in the slightest.

But a promise was a promise. She was dressed and waiting for him when he called at the flat on Sunday and listened with every appearance of interest to the account of the week's work with which he regaled her as they walked to the nearest bus-stop. The concert was in a rather pokey hall and given by an ensemble who played modern music which she didn't like. Frederick sat back with his eyes closed, enjoying it, while she sat beside him, making a mental list of the groceries she would need for the following week and brooding over the patients she would be working on. She clapped when everyone else did and finally rose with well-concealed thankfulness and filed out in to the late April evening. It would be glorious to be at home now, she thought, but here in the busy London street there was only a strip of sky and stars to be seen. She sighed and agreed with Frederick that a cup of coffee would be very nice.

There weren't many cafés open in that part of London on a Sunday evening; the one they entered was small and rather dark and almost empty, but the coffee was good. She accepted a second cup and waited for Frederick to tell her what he so obviously was longing to say. Finally she said, 'There's something on your mind, Frederick. Do tell.'

He said rather pompously. 'Have you ever taken me seriously, Claribel?'

He sounded anxious and she said soothingly, 'No, Frederick, but I don't think you ever led me to suppose . . .' she paused delicately, hoping that he would explain.

'Oh, good'. His relief was so obvious that she almost laughed. 'You see, I like you very much, Claribel—at one time I actually considered asking you to marry me—but I met Joyce when I went home a couple of weeks ago.' He added solemnly, 'I'm not a man to play fast and loose.'

'No, of course you aren't,' she told him warmly. 'I've always considered you as a friend, Frederick, nothing more.' Which wasn't true, but it was what he wanted to hear. 'Tell me about her—does she love you, too?'

'Well I think so, but it's too soon to ask her . . .'

'Rubbish,' cried Claribel. 'How will you ever know if you don't ask? When are you going home again?'

'I've a couple of days due next week.'

'Oh, good. Get after her fast, Frederick, before someone else snaps her up. What is she like?' It took a considerable time to tell her. They had to have a third cup of coffee while he enlarged on the subject nearest his heart.

'Of course, we'll still be real friends?'

She put down her cup for the last time. 'Of course—why ever not? But do let me know what happens, Frederick. I think it's marvellous for you.'

Back in her flat she got supper, fed the cats and sat down to write a letter home. She wouldn't miss Frederick in the least, so why did she feel so out of spirits?

The cats, when questioned, had no answer; she made a pot of tea and went to bed.

Normally a contented girl, sensible enough to accept her lot in life and be happy with it, for after all, it wasn't so bad, Claribel found that her spirits didn't rise. The week went by, busy as it always was, but there were things which should have made her happy. The weather, usually unpredictable in April, had been steadily warmer and sunnier each day so that going to work was a pleasure, even though her way led her through rather shabby streets. Besides, the early tulips in the tubs she had so carefully cherished by the front door had bloomed and gave a nice splash of colour to her little home, and, over and above these small pleasures, she had been given an unexpected free afternoon and had gone shopping. She hadn't intended to buy anything but the sight of a cotton jersey ensemble in a pale toffee colour sent prudence to the winds. She bought it, knowing that its colour did all the right things to her eyes and hair, and this despite the doubt as to when she would be able to wear it. It was too elegant to wear to work and she supposed that she would wear it when she went home for the weekend. Strangely, when one of the house doctors waylaid her on the following afternoon and asked her to spend the following Sunday afteroon with him—an excellent opportunity to air the new outfit—she refused; he was quite a pleasant man but when he suggested that they might go to an absent friend's flat for tea, she prudently said no.

Squashed on the bus going home after this encounter she supposed that she was getting prudish, certainly old-fashioned. Perhaps she should have tried harder with Frederick and made sure of a secure future. She frowned at the thought and an elderly man on whom she had bent her unseeing gaze looked the other way. She wasn't a very nice girl, she reflected, and sighed loudly, right down the neck of the woman pressed against her. The woman turned an indignant face to her. 'Do you mind?' she asked aggressively.

'So sorry,' said Claribel and brought her thoughts back to the present. She got off at the next stop, walked briskly down Meadow Road and unlocked her front door. She felt better once she was inside, with the cats there to welcome her and the prospect of tea.

She cast about her for ways in which to fill the approaching weekend. She could have gone home, but the outfit had cost far too much money; it was pay day during the next week; she would go on the following weekend. She cheered up at the thought and decided to wash the sitting-room net curtains; they were necessary to keep prying eyes from staring in, but they didn't stay clean for more than a week or so. And she would recover the little chair in the bedroom. She had bought the velvet weeks ago and there was webbing and tacks and a hammer somewhere in the kitchen, and while she was at it she could use the rest of the velvet to cover a couple of cushions.

'I'm getting to be a real old maid,' she told the cats.

The weekend came; she had the curtains washed and dripping over the bath and, fired with a sudden energy, had upended the bedroom chair and was ripping off its old cover when there was a thump on the door knocker. It was the kind of thump Mr van Borsele gave. Just for a split second she felt delight surge though her, to be instantly quenched by common sense; he was in Holland.

Only he wasn't. He was on her doorstep, looking impatient when she opened the door.

She stared up at him, conscious of vexation because she was wearing an old dress and a plastic pinny with 'Work Hard' printed on its bib.

'You're in Holland.' she greeted him.

'No, I'm here waiting to be asked in.'

She mumbled, 'Oh, sorry.' How like him to turn a situation to his advantage. 'Do come in, I'm having a weekend turn out.'

He stalked past her. 'Have you nothing better to do?' he asked testily. He poked at the chair. 'Do you know how to upholster chairs as well as get bones working again?'

'No, and I'm not upholstering, only covering. Sit down, Mr van Borsele.'

It would hardly do to ask him why he had come. Instead she asked, 'Would you like some coffee?'

'Yes. I came on the night ferry to Harwich. For some reason there was a hitch and there was no breakfast car on the boat train and I didn't stop on the way.'

Her motherly instincts were aroused. 'Just you sit there and I'll get you a meal. Bacon and eggs and mushrooms and toast and marmalade and tea—no coffee.'

'Since I am in England, a pot of your strong tea and with luck while you are getting it I will see to this chair. It seems as if you are not making a very good job of it.'

She rounded on him indignantly. 'Well, you really are the limit! You come here for breakfast—and there's no reason why I should cook it for you only I've got a kind heart—and then you mock my work. I'd like to see you do it better.'

'And so you shall, Claribel. But I do beg of you, give me a meal before you deliver the lecture which I feel is hovering on your tongue.'

'Oh, you are impossible!' she told him. But she went into the kitchen and got out the jar of fat and the frying pan, and presently the delicious smell of bacon frying filled the little flat.

When she went back into the sitting-room to lay the table she was surprised to see that he had taken off his jacket and was making a splendid job of covering the chair. 'There's no need,' she cried. 'I've all the weekend in which to do it.'

'No you haven't. We're going to Richmond Park after lunch—I need a good brisk walk—and this evening I thought we might go dancing after dinner.'

She stood goggling until he said briskly, 'Don't burn the bacon, Claribel.'

She dished up a plateful, carried it in and set it on the table.

'I don't know what you are talking about,' she began.

'Well, for a start, for heaven's sake stop calling me Mr van Borsele— my name's Marc. You know that already.' He pulled the velvet tight over the chair and tacked it neatly.

He polished off his breakfast and returned to the chair. Claribel, speechless, for she had no idea of how to deal with the situation, cleared away the remnants of his meal, washed the dishes and went back into the sitting-room. The chair was finished, and very nice it looked, too.

'Do passers-by always stare in so rudely?' he wanted to know.

'I've washed the curtains. They're almost dry.'

'Let us hang them up at once then.' Still bemused, she fetched them and watched him hang them up once more. 'And let us hope that is the extent of your activities for the day,' he commented.

She said feebly, 'I'm going to cover some cushions . . .'

'Surely not urgent?' He had settled into an easy chair. 'Get yourself dressed, Claribel, while I take a nap.'

She knew exactly how a rabbit felt when it was face to face with a snake. 'But I'm not going out—I told you . . .'

He stretched out his legs and closed his eyes. 'I haven't come all this way just to watch you do the housework,' he pointed out. 'You have no need to demonstrate your capabilities in that field.'

She stood and looked at him, mulling over a number of things she intended to say, but was stopped from doing this by the quite genuine snore which, while not detracting in the least from his dignity, bore witness to the fact that he was sound asleep.

She stood uncertainly, studying his sleeping face. Very handsome, she conceded, and somehow rather endearing; she almost liked him. She corrected herself: she did like him. His ill-humour didn't mean a thing to her; behind that bland mocking façade there was quite a nice man, she felt sure. She couldn't for the life of her imagine why he had come back to London, but then she knew nothing of his life, did she? And a walk in Richmond Park would really be rather nice . . .

She slid away to her bedroom and got into the new jersey outfit.

CHAPTER FOUR

MR VAN BORSELE was wide awake when she went back into the sitting-room, with the cats on his knee and a rather smug look upon his handsome features. He got up as she went in, remarking that there she was, and that she had been rather a long time, in the manner of someone who had been waiting with impatience, his eye on the clock.

'You were asleep,' said Claribel, quick to point out the fact, 'so don't try and pretend that I've kept you waiting.'

'My dear Claribel, you are the very last person I would pretend to. Are we ready?'

He arranged the cats on the chair he had just vacated and opened the door for her. The Rolls was outside, looking rather out of place in the shabby little road. She cast her eyes back at her windows and was pleased to see the pristine whiteness of the curtains and the tubs of flowers. He followed her look. 'Very nice,' he observed. 'I like your outfit. Did you buy it to wear when you come out with me?'

This perfectly preposterous suggestion left her speechless. She allowed herself to be ushered into the car and the door closed, but she was still speechless when he got in beside her. She said, finally and coldly, 'I bought it because I needed something to wear and I liked it. I had no idea that I should see you again.'

'You hoped you would?' He smiled at her slowly, his head a little on one side.

Claribel opened her handbag, looked inside and closed it up again. 'Well, it's always nice to renew acquaintance with people one has met.' That sounded pompous and affected. 'It's nice to see you again.'

Mr van Borsele let out a long sigh. 'Oh good. Let's have lunch.' He took her to Boulestin's where she ate a delicious lunch which she allowed him to choose for her: chicken mousseline for starters, brill with lobster sauce and chocolate ice-cream in a pastry case.

They didn't linger over their coffee; the bright, sunny afternoon reminded them that they were to visit Richmond Park. On the best of terms, they got back into the car and drove the short distance to the park, left the car and started their walk. They had left the car at the southern edge of the park and were making for Richmond Hill when they paused to admire the view.

'It's nice here,' observed Claribel. 'London seems far away.'

'You don't like London?' He was leaning on a rough wall beside her.

'Well, I like theatres and going out, but only now and again. Life's always such a rush. At home the days seem twice as long.'

She glanced at his face, half turned away from her. 'Do you like London?'

'Just as you do—not too often; but of course, I go where my work takes me.'

'Surely you can choose. Miss Flute said that you were at the top of the tree.'

He laughed. 'It's not much use perching at the top if you're wanted in the branches, is it?'

'So you can't live exactly as you would like?'

'Perhaps not. My work is important to me, of course, but I dare say once I settle down I shall draw in my horns a little.'

They started back presently, and when they were within sight of the car Claribel asked, 'Would you like to come back for tea? It's been a lovely afternoon.'

'Delightful, and yes, I'd like to have tea with you.' He sounded casually friendly.

She offered him the easy chair again, fed the cats and laid the tea tray. A plate of very thin bread and butter, some of her mother's homemade jam and a cake she had baked the previous evening. She carried the tray into the sitting-room and found him asleep again, and waited patiently for several minutes before he opened his eyes.

'Didn't you go to bed last night?' she asked. 'On the ferry, I mean.'

'Oh, yes, for an hour or so. I've had several busy nights and they've caught up with me.'

She gave him tea and a plate and offered him the bread and butter.

'You should have gone to bed and slept the moment you got to London,' she told him severely. 'Do you have to go to Jerome's tomorrow?' She frowned. 'It's Sunday.'

'Certainly not. I've given myself the weekend off.' He made short work of the bread and butter. 'We'll go out to dinner this evening and go dancing.'

'Don't be silly,' she cried. 'You're worn out—I must have been mad to agree to walking all those miles this afternoon. Mr van Borsele . . .' She caught his dark gaze. 'Marc, then—you must drive straight to your hotel and sleep the clock round.'

'I haven't a hotel, and if I sleep the clock round I won't be able to go out this evening, and just now and again, dear girl, it's good to be a little mad.' He sat back in his chair and smiled at her. 'Did you make that cake?'

'Yes, or course I did. Why haven't you a hotel to go to?'

'I have a small flat I use when I come over here.'

She offered him a slice of cake, biting back the questions on her tongue; where was the flat and was it his or lent to him, and was there someone there to look after him? A housekeeper? A girl perhaps? But he had said that he was looking forward to being a family man . . .

His dark eyes were filled with amusement. 'You should learn to disguise your thoughts, Claribel. This is excellent cake. May I call for you at eight o'clock?'

'Well, all right.' That sounded ungracious so she added, 'Thank you, but somewhere quiet, and no dancing. You should have an early night.'

'You're a bossy young woman, Claribel; with a name like that you should be soft and clinging and agree with every word I utter.'

She nodded. 'I told you that was the kind of wife you needed.'

He smiled a little and got to his feet. 'I'll be here at eight o'clock; we'll dine at the Savoy and dance afterwards.' The smile turned to a grin. 'Perhaps it will be my last fling before I marry.'

He paused at the door. 'A delicious tea. Many thanks, Claribel.'

He closed the door quietly behind him and she stood at her window, looking up into the street and watched the Rolls slide away. She began to tidy away the tea things, voicing her thoughts to the cats. 'I can't think why he came here—he must know heaps of girls. And why come to

England when he's got a perfectly good country of his own? And where's this girl he's going to marry?'

She began to wash up, stopping to think from time to time until a glance at the clock sent her scurrying to her wardrobe to find a suitable dress.

There was no time after that; Enoch and Toots wanted their suppers and she stood for ages trying to decide what to wear.

Finally she decided on the newest of her three long dresses, a pearly grey crêpe-de-Chine with a flowery pattern of palest pink and equally pale green. There was no time to wash her hair; she took a shower and dressed and then sat down before her dressing-table and put on her make-up very carefully. She didn't use much. She had a lovely clear skin and thick dark brown lashes which everyone believed she had dyed; cream and powder and a pale pink lipstick were all that she needed. She spent much longer on her hair, arranging it in a coil at the nape of her neck. It added dignity to her appearance, or so she believed.

She was transferring her keys to her evening bag when Mr van Borsele thumped the door knocker. She padded across the room into the tiny hallway and opened the door, to be met by his frosty, 'How many times must I tell you not to open the door unless you have put up the chain? And why are you not wearing any shoes?'

She eyed his magnificent person; she doubted if the inhabitants of Meadow Road had ever seen such dinner-jacketed elegance. She said kindly, 'Goodness, you are cross—but it's your own fault if you won't go to bed and have a good sleep.' She led the way into the living-room. 'And I haven't forgotten my slippers; I'm quite ready.'

She poked her feet into green slippers and picked up

the short velvet evening coat, inherited from an aunt who no longer wore it—its old-fashioned cut had gone full circle and it was once again in the forefront of fashion. Mr van Borsele took it from her and helped her into it and then touched her hair lightly.

'Nice hair,' he commented; Claribel had the depressing feeling that he would have used such a tone of voice if he had been admiring a friend's dog.

There was a good deal of curtain-twitching as they got into the Rolls, but Claribel wasn't disturbed by that. On the whole, she was liked by her immediate neighbours; she was quiet, was meticulous about putting out the rubbish on a Monday morning and never stock-piled empty milk bottles. Nor did she complain when the noisy family across the road gave one of their frequent all-night parties, and when the old lady next door lost her cat it was Claribel who gave up her evening to search the nearby streets and find it. All the same, she found herself reflecting, there would be gossip; Mr van Borsele was becoming a frequent visitor.

The thought became a question. 'Just why did you come to London? You said you had been busy and yet when you get a weekend free you waste half of it travelling.'

He turned to look at her, his eyebrows lifted, a faintly mocking smile on his firm mouth and she went a bright pink. 'Sorry,' she said breathlessly, 'it's none of my business.'

'No, it isn't, Claribel.' He started the car and they purred the length of the dreary road; he didn't speak until they were on the other side of the river. 'Tell me,' he asked, 'do you begin to like me?'

She said crossly, 'You do ask such awkward questions, but since you ask, yes, most of the time I like you.'

She drew a deep breath. 'Though why that matters I can't think.'

'Pretty girls like you shouldn't think too much. Shall we agree to like each other just for this evening? Such a pity to come all this way . . .' He left the rest of his remark in the air.

She smoothed her silken lap. 'Why not?' She felt bewildered. She was a level-headed girl, leading a well-ordered life, but now, suddenly, she felt reckless. 'I—I think I'm going to enjoy my evening.'

'I know I am.' He ran the car down the entrance to the Savoy, handed it over to the doorman and ushered her inside.

The River Room was almost full, but their table was one of the best in the room, in one of the windows, overlooking the Embankment. Claribel, more than ready to enjoy herself, beamed at her companion. 'This is simply super,' she told him. 'Have you got hotels like this in Holland?'

'In the big cities, yes. Where I live there is very little night life, though Holland is a small country and it is possible to spend an evening out without having to drive too far.'

She chose smoked salmon, chicken cooked in a cream sauce and an omelette filled with strawberries and awash with a wine sauce and thick cream. Mr van Borsele ate his fillet steak and then suggested that they might dance.

Claribel was a good dancer, but then so was he; they suited each other perfectly and although the omelette was delicious she got to her feet at once when he suggested that they might dance again. He had contented himself with the cheeseboard, and when they got back to their table coffee was brought at once. Claribel poured out. 'Oh, I am enjoying myself,' she declared, and presently they danced again. They danced until late, but not too late to stop quite a few curtains twitching as he pushed open her door for her and bade her goodnight.

'I'll be here at ten o'clock tomorrow,' he observed as she paused uncertainly in the doorway. 'Goodnight, Claribel.' He edged her gently inside, shut the door on her, got back into his car and drove away.

'Well, whatever next?' asked Claribel of the cats. 'Ten o'clock indeed, and just what did that mean? For two pins I'll be in bed . . . Anyone would suppose that he was anxious to be rid of me.' She began to undress slowly. 'I don't have to go out with him again, do I?' she wanted to know, but both cats had curled up at the end of the bed and took no notice.

A brilliantly sunny morning melted her stern resolutions of the night before. She was up early to feed the cats, eat her breakfast, tidy her small home, and dress with care in the new outfit once more. She was sitting, apparently doing nothing, when Mr van Borsele arrived, to bang on her door with his customary vigour. His 'Hello—coffee?' quite put her off her stroke. She had planned to be cool and casual and here he was demanding coffee the moment he poked his commanding nose around her door.

'Do sit down,' she begged him coldly, 'while I make the coffee.' She swept into the kitchen and filled the kettle with a good deal of noise and clattered the mugs on to the tray.

'The peace of domesticity,' he observed from the comfort of his chair. The cats were squashed on to either side of him and he had his eyes closed.

Claribel peered at him round the kitchen door. 'Domesticity has two sides to it,' she pointed out rather sharply. 'You have overlooked the cooking and washing up and clearing away side of it.'

'No, no.' He opened an eye to look at her. 'There is pleasure in the sight of some little woman bending over the kitchen sink.'

Claribel said 'Huh!' Had he noticed that she wasn't a little woman and she loathed washing up? She retired to the kitchen before he could answer that.

She offered him his coffee and passed the sugar without speaking and went to sit on the little spinning-chair by the window.

'The Cotswolds?' He sounded almost humble, although she suspected him of being nothing of the sort.

'Too far.'

'Nonsense. We'll go through Twyford and Didcot and through the White Horse Vale and have bread and cheese in Adlestrop . . .'

'But that's almost in Cheltenham—it's miles away.'

'A change of scene is good for one.' He finished his coffee. 'Drink up, Claribel. Feed your cats and bolt your windows and turn off the gas and do the hundred-and-one things women do before they go out.'

She rounded on him. 'The first thing you said when you got here was "Coffee?" and now I'm expected to rush and tear around at the drop of a hat.'

He got up, his head almost towering to the ceiling. 'I'll see to these mugs and feed the cats; you go and comb your golden hair.' And, when she put a hand up to her hair, 'I speak metaphorically.'

There wasn't a great deal of traffic once they had shaken off London and its suburbs, and Mr van Borsele kept to the secondary roads as far as possible, driving with a nonchalant ease which Claribel, a rather nervous driver herself, envied.

They talked comfortably and sometimes lapsed into companionable silences, while the Rolls sped effortlessly towards Adlestrop which when they reached it was quite delightful, with its houses of golden stone and the cottages lining the main street with dormer windows and weathered slate roofs. Mr van Borsele slid to a halt in the courtyard of the village pub and helped Claribel out of the car.

'I've been here before,' he told her. 'I think you will like it.'

She did. The bar was long and rather dark, held together by crooked beams and yellowed plaster walls; there was a darts board at one end, but thankfully no fruit machines or taped music. There were a lot of people there; church was over and it wanted ten minutes before the one o'clock Sunday dinner would be dished up in almost every home in the village. She was settled at a table, asked what she would like to drink and given the menu card from the bar, unaware of the admiring glances sent her way. Mr van Borsele came back with her drink and a tankard of beer for himself and they discussed what they should eat. 'You said bread and cheese,' she glanced at him, smiling, 'so I'll have a ploughman's lunch—with stilton.'

The food when it came was delicious: homemade bread, a little pat of butter in a pot and a generous wedge of cheese with an array of pickles. They ate with appetite and finished with coffee before Mr van Borsele suggested that they might stroll through the village and take a look at the church.

They wandered round, looking at the numerous monuments to the Leigh family who had lived in the great house nearby for hundreds of years. Some of the inscriptions were very old and Mr van Borsele obligingly translated their Latin text. Claribel, listening to his deep voice, reflected that if he had been Frederick she would have been bored; as it was, she wished the day to last for twice its usual length.

A wish she was not granted. They had wandered out of the church into the sunshine again and Mr van Borsele said, 'Ah, well, a delightful interlude—now for home.'

Claribel had allowed her thoughts to dwell on tea at some wayside cottage and perhaps dinner that evening, but she agreed at once; perhaps he had had enough of her company, even though he had made such a point of spending the day with her. The thought caused her conversation to become rather stiff and her companion smiled once or twice, remarking casually that they would go back through Chipping Norton and join the road to Oxford. 'We can pick up the motorway there,' he explained. 'It's barely an hour's run from there to London. Will you give me tea when we get back?'

'Of course.' She spoke in her best hostess voice and his dark eyes gleamed with amusement.

It was just after five o'clock when he opened her door and she went into the living-room. The cats rushed to meet them as she opened the kitchen window to let them into the tiny back yard before she put on the kettle. There were the biscuits she had baked earlier in the week and the rest of the cake; she got the tray ready and carried it through and poured the tea.

'Thank you for my lovely day,' she said politely. 'I really enjoyed it.'

'But you are wondering why I have brought you back

without so much as stopping for tea—you may even have wondered if I was going to ask you out to dinner?' His voice was bland. 'Unfortunately I have to go back to Holland this evening.'

She tumbled her cup on to its saucer and almost broke it. 'You what? This evening? But it's almost six o'clock now; why didn't you tell me?'

'You sound like a wife.' He was laughing at her. 'If I had told you it would altogether have spoilt your day; you would have been looking at your watch every ten minutes.' He sat looking at her for a long moment. 'You know, Claribel, you are the only girl I know who doesn't bore me; you eat bread and cheese and inspect churches and don't fidget with your hair and make-up and you make an excellent cup of coffee and yet you make any man proud to take you out to dinner.'

She stared back at him. 'Why did you come?'

He got to his feet. 'My dear Claribel, I have just told you. Thank you for my tea. Your biscuits melt in the mouth. *Tot ziens.*'

She was at the door with him. 'What does that mean?'

'In this case, until I see you again.'

'Don't be too sure of that.' She gave him a frosty smile and offered a polite hand. It was disconcerting to have it held gently and then kissed.

She watched him drive away, shut the door smartly and poured herself another cup of tea. 'I didn't like him when we met,' she told the cats, 'and then I did, or I thought I did, but I don't. And if he thinks I'll give him biscuits next time he comes, he's in for a disappointment—dry bread and water.' Her voice rose indignantly. 'I shan't open the door.'

But while washing up it crossed her mind that it wasn't

very likely that he would come again. She had been far too easy with him; she should have refused his first invitation. He was unsettling—not her type . . . She said it twice out loud to make sure that she believed it.

So she should have been glad that there was no sign of him, let alone mention of his name, during the ensuing week. She had decided to go home for the weekend but instead of going on the Friday evening, she told herself that there was no rush; she caught a mid-morning train on the Saturday, refusing to admit to herself that she had been hoping for Mr van Borsele's imperious thump on her door.

'You're pale, dear,' observed her mother. 'You've been working too hard, cooped up in London; I hope you get into the parks at the weekends. Does that solemn young man—Frederick wasn't it?—still walk you miles on Sundays?'

'No, Mother—he's going to marry a girl he met when he went home a month or so ago.'

'Oh, do you mind, darling?' Her mother was bending over the tapestry frame she worked at with religious persistence.

'Not a bit.'

'Oh, good. I never thought that he was quite the right man for you. Do you see anything of that nice man who gave you a lift here?'

'He is Dutch, mother dear; he lives in Holland. He comes over to Jerome's to operate from time to time.'

Her mother eyed her narrowly. Dear Claribel wasn't fibbing, but she was holding something back. Mrs Brown allowed herself a small smug smile. She was a firm believer in motherly instinct, and so far it had never let her down.

She made no demur when dear Claribel decided that she

would have to go back to Meadow Road by an earlier train than usual. Things to do, she had said vaguely, smalls to wash and she simply *had* to turn out the kitchen cupboard. Her mother agreed soothingly, packed up a pot of homemade marmalade and a rich fruit cake and begged her not to work too hard. 'Have fun, too,' she advised. 'I'm sure you get lots of dates.'

Claribel agreed, as indeed she did—but she didn't always accept them.

Monday morning began all wrong; she woke late, her hair refused to go up with its usual smoothness, the cats didn't want to come in from the yard and she broke a plate, then to crown it all she missed her bus. She got to Jerome's out of breath, a little peevish and with a heightened colour.

'Late,' observed Miss Flute, 'but not too late to go the men's ward—Mr Shutter's round.'

Claribel cheered up at once. The wards were interesting; the patients she had to treat there were suffering from complicated broken bones which it gave her great pleasure to straighten out again. She sped through the hospital and reached the group of people gathered round Sister just as the clock struck the hour.

They were just inside the ward doors and as they swung open Sister stepped forward; it was her perogative to say good morning before anyone else. But it wasn't Mr Shutter who answered it. Mr van Borsele, followed by another group, this time the registrar, houseman and students, strode through the door, acknowledged her greeting with a courteous smile and cast his eyes over her entourage. Claribel had gone a good deal pinker than she already was by reason of her haste and his gaze paused momentarily at her astonished face and then swept on without any sign of recognition. Not that he could have said anything, but a smile would have been quite permissible. The day had begun badly, she reflected, and it looked likely to continue so. She submerged herself among the nurses and the lady social worker, no easy task since her splendid person made the rest of them look like midgets, and she followed dutifully in the wake of Mr van Borsele and his team. She wasn't left long in obscurity, though; she had been treating several of the patients and Mr van Borsele wished to see what progress had been made, so she lifted arms and legs, demonstrated the head traction on one unfortunate young man who had had a fracture of his cervical spine, and then assisted an elderly man to demonstrate his walking powers.

'Very nice,' commented Mr van Borsele in measured tones. 'Shall we see this patient Mr Shutter has told me of? He's for theatre this afternoon. Miss Brown, you will begin passive exercises as soon as he is conscious—he is unfortunately a chronic bronchial but if we are to save that leg we must operate immediately. So breathing exercises and hourly coughing, if you please.' His glance was impersonal.

He left the ward presently and, after a brief consultation with Sister, Claribel went back to the physio department, where she poked her bright head round Miss Flute's door. 'May I come in? I say, I've been given that man who came in last night with the compound fracture of the left leg. He's a chest as well; I have to give him hourly treatment starting when he's in recovery coming round from the anaesthetic—that'll be late afternoon, I suppose. And I'm booked solid down here.'

Miss Flute looked unworried. 'Yes, dear, I'll have to transfer your patients for a day or two. Someone will take over for night duty? What hours have you got, did anyone tell you?'

'Sister asked me to stay until eight this evening; she said she'd be seeing you.' Claribel paused. 'It's a bit awkward—the cats, you know.'

Miss Flute, who had an elderly moggie herself, nodded sympathetically. 'Suppose you go home about three o'clock—you can be back before five o'clock? The list doesn't start until three o'clock; I should think you won't be needed for a couple of hours.' The phone rang and she stopped to answer it, nodding her head and saying yes, yes, several times.

'Sister,' she told Claribel. 'Would you like to do eight in the morning till half past four; she can have Mrs Down from then until eight o'clock and I'll do the night shift.' And, when Claribel lightly protested, 'No, don't argue, Miss Brookes can hold the fort here until midday, when Mrs Green can come on duty here until she relieves you. It will only be for a few days; once we've got him going it will be a TDS job. We've done this before, there's no reason why it won't work again.'

Miss Flute's word was law. Claribel, after a hurried return to her flat to see Enoch and Toots, presented herself in Intensive Care to wait for the arrival of the patient. He came from the recovery room with two nurses in attendance and for the first hour there was nothing for her to do except watch the nurses hoist the plastered leg on to a Balkan beam and apply the weights. A very nasty compound fracture, one of them told her; bits of bone all over the place, but Mr van Borsele had assembled them with infinite patience, pinned them neatly, nailed the bone together and was of the opinion that the leg would be quite useful in a few months' time. The leg, at the moment, looked of no use at all, with toes sticking out of the foot end of the plaster and a long window cut so that the big incision which had been made could be examined frequently.

Presently the man opened his eyes and Claribel started her work. He certainly had what she would have described as a nasty chest, but he had no wish to cough.

'Oh, come now,' said Claribel at her most beguiling. 'You're going to feel so much better, and that's a promise. It's no good you arguing, for I have to do this every hour, but the more you cough the quicker I'll stop plaguing you.'

The man swore softly but he did as she asked and presently lay back on his pillows while the nurses made him more comfortable.

'Everything all right?' asked Mr van Borsele in her ear. 'If you can keep that up for a couple of days he'll be OK.' He went past her to bend over his patient and then went away again as quietly as he had come.

Miss Flute came just as quietly at eight o'clock, nodded briskly to Claribel, exchanged a few knowledgeable remarks and bade her go home just as Mr van Borsele returned, so there was a small delay while Claribel gave her report and, when she would have gone, 'Wait for me, if you please, Miss Brown.' His voice was pleasant but held a note which she didn't care to ignore. She went to stand with Miss Flute while he conferred with the night nurse and Sister, took another look at his patient and rejoined them to wish Miss Flute goodnight and urge Claribel through the door.

In the corridor he said briefly, 'I'll be outside the physio department entrance in five minutes. I'll run you home.'

'Thank you, but there is no need. I'm perfectly able . . .'

'Don't argue, Claribel; we're both tired and you need a

night's sleep—I want that man fit in the shortest possible time.'

She said, 'Very well, Mr van Borsele,' in such a meek voice that he opened his eyes wide although he said nothing. They went down in the lift to the ground floor and parted without a word.

She was tired; she hadn't realised that until now. The patient was a heavy man and unwilling, and he had been hard work; supper and bed would be delightful. She changed and locked the door after her and found the Rolls waiting. Mr van Borsele, lounging over its bonnet, opened the door for her, got in and drove away without speaking. There wasn't a great deal of traffic and Meadow Road when they reached it was deserted. He got out when she did, took her key and opened the door and followed her inside.

'Coffee?' asked Claribel, anticipating what he was going to say.

'No, tea, I think. And a sandwich?' He went past her and put the kettle on. 'Hello, Claribel.'

She turned to stare at him. 'But you saw me this morning . . .'

'So I did, but that was—how shall I put it?—a professional meeting. Now we are just you and me.'

He watched her face, reading her thoughts. 'The last thing I would wish to do would be to lay you open to the hospital grapevine.' He took the teapot from her and poured hot water into it. 'I value your friendship too much.'

She stood there watching him empty the teapot, spoon in tea and pour on the boiling water. 'You don't seem like a friend,' she muttered. 'Oh, you're very kind, giving me lifts and—and a day out and dinner . . . but I don't understand you. Sometimes I'm not sure if I like you.'

'I know that. Don't let it worry you.' He smiled suddenly

at her and she saw then that he was tired. She said quite sharply, 'Do sit down; I'll make those sandwiches. Do you have to go back to Jerome's?'

'In an hour or so, yes.' He lounged back in his chair and closed his eyes and she felt a sharp pang of pity as she got out the bread and butter and started on the sandwiches. He hadn't stirred when she had finished so she fed the cats and carried the tray noiselessly into the living-room. He needed a good hot meal, she thought worriedly; probably he hadn't had lunch and would forget about his dinner if he was worried about his patient. He was a man who drove himself too hard.

She piled sandwiches on a plate and poured the tea, and when she turned round he was watching her closely; there was nothing sleepy about his gaze.

She said tartly, 'I thought you were asleep.'

'I was. What is in the sandwiches?'

'Cheese and pickles, ham, lettuce and tomato.'

He munched contentedly. 'Tell, me, Claribel, when you marry will you be prepared to offer your husband refreshment at whatever hour he comes home?'

'Well, of course, provided he's been working and not just gallivanting around.'

He said seriously, 'I can't imagine your marrying a man who gallivanted. These sandwiches are delicious.'

'Didn't you have any lunch?'

'No.' He took another sandwich and bit into it.

'But you'll get dinner when you get back to Jerome's?'

'Probably. It depends on how that man is doing. You take over in the morning?'

'At eight o'clock. What kind of a chance has he?'

They talked comfortably about the case and presently

he got up to go.

He wasted no words on polite observations that he would see her in the morning or anything similar, merely bade her goodnight, adding a laconic, 'Thanks for the food, Claribel.'

Leaving her, as he usually did, feeling cross.

She saw him frequently during the next day or two but only on the ward, and then to do no more than pass her report to whichever nurse was on duty.

The patient was hard work, but he was responding at last; by the third day Claribel no longer needed to be with him continuously. Miss Flute went back to her office and Claribel and Mrs Green shared a complicated schedule of duty for another thirty-six hours before he was pronounced out of danger and needed physiotherapy only morning and evening, so that he could be fitted in with her other ward cases.

It would be nice to be back to normal working conditions, Claribel assured Miss Flute, while at the back of her mind there was regret at not seeing Mr van Borsele again. And when the following day she went to the ward for a round, it was Mr Shutter who arrived to take it. Gone back to Holland, ruminated Claribel, busy showing Mr Shutter just how nicely a boy with cut tendons of the hand had regained very nearly its full powers. Not that she missed him, but he could have said goodbye.

She was going home for the weekend; she raced to the flat as the buses were slow, gobbling her tea, showered and changed, fed the cats and ushered them to their basket. With luck she might just catch the train before her usual one. She was dashing about on a last-minute check when the door knocker was thumped. The sound brought her up short; only one person used such force and he, to the best of her knowledge, was in Holland.

He was on the doorstep. She drew a breath. 'I'm just leaving . . .'

'The warmth of your welcome leaves much to be desired,' he observed mildly. 'All the same, I shall come in.'

Which he did, shoving her gently ahead of him until they were both in the living-room.

She turned to face him. 'Look, I'm catching a train home—I shall miss it!'

'I'll drive you down—I'm going that way.' He gave her a beguiling smile. 'We could have a cup of coffee now and I'll give you dinner on the way.'

'Mother's expecting me.'

He lifted the receiver off the cradle and handed it to her. 'I'll put the kettle on.' He went into the kitchen, unfastening the cat's basket as he went, leaving her speechless. She put the receiver back and followed him into the kitchen. 'Look, this really is too much; you walk in here and tell me what to do, and now I've missed my train!'

He was spooning coffee into two mugs. 'We'll get there before the train or very soon after.' He added blandly, 'Shouldn't you let your mother know?'

She went back to the telephone and rang her mother, aware that she was taking the line of least resistance. Her temper wasn't improved by her mother's cheerful voice. 'How nice, dear. Your father and I both hoped that we'd meet your nice young man again . . .'

'He's not my young man.' She spoke in a cross rather loud voice and put the receiver down quite sharply.

'Is it so refreshing,' remarked Mr van Borsele from the kitchen, 'to be referred to as a young man, even when the speaker is now in a nasty temper.'

He handed her a mug of coffee with a disarming smile and she found her peevishness evaporating. She said, half laughing, 'Doesn't anything upset you?'

'Oh, yes.'

He was quite serious. He sat down in the easy chair and sipped his coffee and, because she found the silence a little awkward, she asked, 'Are you over here to work again?'

He nodded. 'We shall change that plaster—I think I may close the wound; he's doing extremely well. And there's a rather complicated case Mr Shutter has asked me to discuss.'

'Don't you mind going to and fro so often? Don't you want to be at home?'

'Do you not have a saying, "Home is where the heart is"?'

She looked at him, puzzled. 'Do you mean that you can't settle down?'

He smiled a little. 'At the moment it would be premature.'

She picked up the mugs and took them to the kitchen. 'You're going to get married, Mr van Borsele?'

'The name is Marc, and yes, that is my intention.'

'Then you won't come over to England so often?' She turned to look at him and met his dark eyes and felt the colour flooding her face when she saw his raised eyebrows. She said gruffly, 'I didn't mean to be nosey.'

She scooped up the cats and put them back into their basket. 'I'm ready when you are.' Her voice was wooden with embarrassment. 'It's kind of you to run me home.' She took a quick peep at him and saw that he was smiling. 'What's so funny?'

He took the basket from her. 'You know, you really are rather a dear girl—you'll make a splendid wife.' He opened the door and she went past him, her question unanswered.

CHAPTER FIVE

IN HER efforts to appear quite at ease, Claribel plunged into talk, trivial stuff to which her companion replied politely without contributing any conversation of his own. After a time her chatter petered out and she sat silent.

Mr van Borsele gave a deep sigh and observed blandly, 'There's no need to try so hard, Claribel. You may not like me overmuch but at least you know me well enough by now to be able to keep silent if you wish. Where shall we stop for a meal?' he asked, but didn't wait for her to answer.

They were almost on to the M3 which would take them nearly as far as Andover. 'Once we are off the motorway we can stop at Middle Wallop—there's a good restaurant there, the Old Drapery Stores, run by a Dutch family.'

He began to talk easily about the place in a placid voice so that presently Claribel began to relax again. By the time they reached the restaurant she was her usual self, able to enjoy the good food set before her. But they didn't linger over the meal; they were on their way again within the hour, speeding towards Salisbury.

'I'll take the A30 and turn off it at Fovant,' observed Mr van Borsele, and he put down his well-shod foot.

It was dark by now but the sky was starlit and the moon was rising; the road leapt ahead of them in the car's powerful headlamps and Claribel, quietly content without quite knowing why, sat back in her seat, watching Mr van Borsele's masterly handling of his car.

They turned off at Fovant, travelling along a narrow country road full of unexpected twists and turns. 'Tell me if I go wrong,' said Mr van Borsele placidly. 'I don't know this road.'

There were no villages, only the odd farmhouse or row of farm cottages and the occasional isolated house standing well back from the road.

Mr van Borsele slowed for an S-bend and as they came out of it slowed still more; there were blue lights flashing ahead of them and a police road sign. A few hundred yards down the road they were stopped by a policemen.

Mr van Borsele opened his window. 'Anything I can do to help, constable?' he asked. 'I'm a doctor.'

'We are waiting for the ambulance, sir—there's a badly injured man and an elderly couple with cuts and shock and a young lady apparently uninjured. If you'd care to take a look at the man? We—we aren't sure . . .' He glanced at Claribel, hesitating.

'This lady is hospital staff and unshockable.' If Mr van Borsele heard her indignant breath he gave no sign. 'I'll have a look if you wish.'

He got out of the car, took his bag off the back seat, said, 'Stay where you are,' to Claribel and walked off with the constable.

He had been gone perhaps ten minutes when the ambulance arrived, but it was a good deal longer than that before he returned. He stuck his head through the window to address her.

'The man is dead. The ambulance will take the other two into Salisbury, but the girl's unhurt and she is desperate to get to Bath as quickly as possible. I'll give her a lift—her family live there.'

He went away again before Claribel could ask any questions and presently returned with the girl, small and slim and dark with an elfin prettiness and an air of helplessness. As they reached the car she stared up into Mr van Borsele's face with what Claribel uncharitably considered to be a sickening look of adoration.

'You're so very kind,' she uttered in a wispy little-girl voice. 'I don't know what I would have done . . .' Her voice faltered and a small sob escaped her. 'I simply must get back home this evening—my parents will be so worried.'

She allowed him to settle her in the back of the car and Mr van Borsele said briskly, 'Claribel, will you get in with this young lady? She's had rather a shock. Do you suppose your mother would give her a cup of tea before I take her on to Bath? She's had a bad time.'

Claribel got out and got in again beside the girl, who threw her a quick look and smiled charmingly.

'Of course,' she agreed at once. 'We could put her up for the night if that would be a good idea.'

She was interrupted instantly by the girl saying urgently, 'No, no, I must be taken home as quickly as possible.' The girl's voice was so urgent that Claribel looked at her in surprise. She said kindly, 'Well, I'm sure if it's urgent that you should go home, Mr van Borsele will take you.'

He had been conferring with the road traffic police but now he came back to his own car.

'The police will contact you in the morning,' he told the girl in what Claribel considered to be far too soothing a manner; couldn't he see that the girl was acting up? She had shown no concern for her dead companion or the couple in the other car and Claribel didn't think she was in a state of shock, either; her colour was good, her hands were as steady as rocks and she had taken out a pocket mirror and was studying her face in it.

Mr van Borsele gave her a long, considering look and got into the car.

'We turn off somewhere here?' he asked Claribel over his shoulder.

'Left at the next signpost.' She sat looking out of the window, worrying a little about the dead man and the elderly couple. 'They'll be all right?' she asked.

He understood her at once. 'Yes. They were on their way to Wilton; they have a son living there. The police will take him to them.'

'And the poor man?'

'His people come from Bath; the police have the address.'

'His poor mother and father,' muttered Claribel. Mr van Borsele didn't answer; the girl ignored her.

Her mother needed only the briefest of explanations before ushering them into the sitting-room, offering a bed to the girl to rest upon, hot tea and the telephone. 'Your parents will be worried,' she said kindly.

'I don't want to phone.' The girl sounded uneasy. 'If I could just have some tea, the doctor has kindly offered to drive me home—I have to get back as soon as possible.'

She flashed a smile at Mrs Brown and allowed herself to be settled in Mr Brown's easy chair. When Claribel came in with the tea tray presently she was talking animatedly to Mr Brown and Mr van Borsele.

As Claribel poured the tea and offered biscuits, Mr van Borsele asked casually, 'This young man who was killed, you knew him well?'

The girl shrugged. 'I've lots of friends. He always drove

too fast.'

Claribel saw the shocked look on her mother's face and made a great business of passing teacups.

Mr van Borsele got up the minute he had finished his tea. 'We'll go, shall we?' he asked and the girl jumped up and hurried to the door, barely pausing to utter thanks. She flashed the smile at Mrs Brown again, another one at Mr Brown, wasted no more than a nod at Claribel and caught Mr van Borsele by the arm. 'I do feel shaky,' she told him in her little-girl voice, and gave him a limpid look.

He bade Mrs Brown goodbye and thanked her without any appearance of haste, shook Mr Brown by the hand and paused by Claribel. 'Have a pleasant weekend,' he advised her. 'I'm sorry it had to start like this.'

Then they had gone. Claribel watched the car's tail-lights disappear into the lane and came in and shut the door. She didn't go back into the sitting-room at once but went to let out the indignant cats and feed them. It was in the kitchen that her mother joined her.

'Tell me about it, love. I know Mr van Borsele gave us the facts but I want the trimmings.' She sat down at the table. 'I didn't like that girl.'

'Nor did I.' Claribel cut a slice of bread from the loaf on the table and began to munch it. 'Mother, she didn't utter one word of concern for that poor man who was killed, and all that "poor little me" act she put on just for Marc's benefit . . . Men!' said Claribel with feeling. 'They can be so dim.'

Mrs Brown had felt a certain satisfaction when Claribel had said 'Marc', but just now it was overshadowed by the memory of the girl. Men, the most sensible of men, fell for that helpless wistful look; it was unfortunate that her darling Claribel had never looked either wistful or helpless; indeed, she was usually the first to come forward with a practical suggestion of help or matter-of-fact solving of a problem. She sighed. 'Perhaps she was in shock', she suggested half-heartedly.

'Oh, pooh!' said Claribel.

Mr van Borsele hadn't said a word about taking her back and, since he hadn't phoned by Sunday morning, she packed her overnight bag again, had lunch with her parents and told them she would go back by train. 'If you wouldn't mind taking me into Tisbury, Father? There's the five-fifteen that'll get me back in nice time for supper.'

Mr Brown had his mouth open to observe that surely Mr van Borsele was calling for her when he encountered his wife's eloquent look. He closed his mouth, coughed and said, 'Of course, dear. That's a good train.'

There was time to go for a quick walk along the bridlepath after lunch. Claribel took Rover with her and tried not to think about Mr van Borsele. Of course, she had never liked him, she reminded herself; it was highly likely that he had only taken her out because there was no one else available. She would, she observed to Rover, accept the invitation she had had from one of the medical housemen to accompany him to a disco at the club the following weekend and in the mean time, if Mr van Borsele should knock on her door, which seemed unlikely, she would on no account open it.

Her mother had tea ready when she got back. She made brisk work of it, reminding her father that he was to drive her to the station and went upstairs to get her bag. She was stowing the cats into their basket when the phone rang. Her mother was standing with her, and Claribel said urgently,

'You answer it, Mother. Just tell Marc if it's him that I've gone back by train,' and, when her mother hesitated, added fiercely, 'Please, Mother. Look, I'll go outside; Father's already in the garage, so you won't be fibbing . . .' She kissed her doubtful parent and darted through the door with the cats and her bag.

To her father's surprised, 'You could have waited indoors, my dear,' she said airily, 'I thought it would save you a minute or two and we haven't all that much time, have we?'

It was absurd, but she didn't feel safe until she was on the train on the way to Salisbury and London. Safe from what? she asked herself. The possibility that Mr van Borsele might have that girl with him? Or that his phone call could have been made from a nearby call-box and he was even now listening to her mother's only too obviously trumped-up excuses.

Claribel sat staring out of the window. Perhaps it hadn't been him at all, in which case there was no harm done. The more she thought about it the more certain she felt this to be the case, and by the time the train got into Waterloo station she had managed to dismiss the whole business from her mind. She took a taxi to the flat, an unwonted luxury, but the buses were full and she had the cats.

Meadow Road was a cruel contrast to the peace of the Wiltshire countryside. She unlocked her door and went inside quickly; at least her own little flat looked cosy and welcoming.

She freed the cats and, since they were grumbling, fed them before she did anything else, but half an hour later she was laying the table for her supper—scrambled eggs on toast and a pot of tea, and since the evenings were still chilly she lit the gas fire, pulled the curtains and turned on the radio—it was something wistful and romantic and suited her mood exactly. She had the saucepan with the butter and the milk heated ready for the eggs when there was a knock at the door. Only one person thumped it in that ferocious manner—Mr van Borsele—and she had promised herself that she wouldn't let him in. A second thunderous knock changed her mind for her; the neighbours, already deeply interested in his comings and goings, would be at their windows twitching their curtains. She went to the door and flung it open, the saucepan still in her hands.

Mr van Borsele scooped her to one side and went past her into the living-room. He said in an admonitory voice, 'Must I remind you yet again not to open the door unless the chain is in position?'

The remark wasn't what she had expected; she gaped at him, speechless. He took the saucepan from her, turned off the gas and set it tidily on the stove.

'Your mother,' he observed in a silky voice, 'is a charming woman—I like her immensely—but she's a very poor fibber. Besides, you banged the front door as you went out.'

Claribel found her voice. 'Go away,' she said loudly. 'I don't know why you're here . . .'

'You fib as badly as your mother. Of course you know why I'm here and I'm not going away. I've driven at risk to life and limb in order to get here before you locked up for the night. Why did you run away?'

'I didn't.' Her voice came out too loud and she tried to keep it cool and dignified. 'I have to go to work in the morning which means that I have to get back here this evening. I caught the train . . .'

His smile disquieted her for it held mockery. 'Now let

me guess—I didn't say that I would take you back; indeed, I went on my way with a charming fairylike creature whose antics were calculated to arouse male chivalry to its highest pitch. Naturally, with two days in which to embroider your imagination to the full, you felt yourself cast off, rejected for a slip of a girl half your size; you probably went for a long walk, vowing never to open your door to me again . . .'

Claribel glared at him; he was so exactly right. She said frostily, 'Don't be so conceited; I've other things to think about,' and added loftily, 'Now do go, I want to cook my supper.' However, she was unable to prevent herself from saying, 'I'm not a bit interested in how you spent your weekend.'

She took a quick look at him. His face was impassive but his eyes were gleaming with amusement. She hadn't liked that bit about the girl being half her size, it made her feel a size eighteen at least, and she wasn't; she was a nicely curved twelve.

His smile had lost its mockery. 'May I stay to supper?' he asked. 'And will you empty that head of yours of the fairy stories you've been thinking up?' He went past her into the kitchen, broke eggs into a bowl and began to beat them with a fork. 'I'll do the eggs if you make the toast.' And, when she began to slice a loaf, still wordless, 'That girl had gone off with the young man who was killed; they were evidently intent on a weekend together and she had told her parents that she was staying with friends. Hence her anxiety to get to Bath—heaven knows what story she cooked up for them. Just as well I didn't accept her invitation to go in provided I said nothing about the accident. I was already late.' He poured the eggs into the saucepan and stirred them very gently. 'I went to see my sister—she had a son on Sunday morning. We were up all night with her, and by the time I got back from the hospital it was early morning, too soon to phone you. I slept for a bit and then went back to see her.'

Claribel stood, her knife poised over the bread, her pretty face the picture of contrition.

'Oh, Marc, I'm a witless fool. I'm so sorry. You've had almost no sleep and now you've come racing back without your supper.'

He said placidly, 'I like driving and I'm going to have my supper and I can always catch up on my sleep. May I use all these eggs?'

'Yes, of course. What would you like to drink?' She had forgotten her peevishness, bent on feeding him, seeing, now that she really looked at him, that he was tired to his bones.

'Tea. Is there anything to drink before supper?'

'Father gave me a bottle of claret months ago. I'll find it.'

She rooted around in the cupboard in the living-room and held up the bottle for his inspection. He nodded approvingly. 'Rather unusual before a meal, but we must celebrate with something.'

'Celebrate? What are we celebrating?'

'Why, that we are back on our old footing, Claribel. If you'll find a corkscrew I will open this.'

While he was doing that, she laid another place at the table, feeling suddenly light-hearted.

They drank their claret—not quite at the right temperature for Mr van Borsele, who was a stickler for such things—buttered quantities of toast, and dished up the eggs. When they had eaten, Claribel fetched the fruit cake her mother had given her and watched her companion eat several large slices, washed down with tea. Finally, he sat back.

'A delightful meal, Claribel.' He glanced at his watch. 'But unfortunately I must go. Forgive me if I don't wash the dishes?'

He had got up and she stood up too, disappointed but determined not to show it. The vague idea that they might have spent the rest of the evening together, sitting comfortably before the fire, talking about nothing much, had taken root in her head; she told herself now that there was no reason why he should do so. On the face of things, she was a bolthole convenient for a quick meal, a kind of younger sister . . . She disliked the idea very much.

'Don't be late,' she said brightly and wondered where he was going—it was almost ten o'clock and a Sunday . . .

He grinned suddenly. 'Claribel, you're making up fairytales again. Why not ask me where I'm going?'

She said severely, 'Certainly not. And in any case I have no wish to pry into your life.'

He tapped her cheek with a gentle finger. 'But we are friends again?'

She said peevishly, 'If by that you mean may you come here for coffee and a meal when you have nowhere better to go, then yes.'

'That's my kind, forgiving girl.' He put out a hand. 'Friends?'

His grip was firm and brief, his nod of goodbye even briefer. When he had driven away she slowly cleared the table, washed up and put her breakfast ready. It was obvious to her that, whether she liked it or not, he regarded her as a sister; the thought was very depressing.

In the morning she viewed things in a different light; common sense asserted itself. There was no reason why Mr van Borsele shouldn't consider her in the light of a sister. He was at liberty to do so if he wished, only somehow she was finding it difficult to look upon him as a brother . . .

She saw him thrice during the week. On the first occasion it was on the ward, during his round, when she was called upon to demonstrate the progress of the patients she had been treating, and two days later there was a lengthy session with the chesty man, now making steady progress despite his wheezing. The third occasion was a rather different one. On Saturday morning she was window-shopping in the Burlington Arcade, looking for a suitable birthday present for her father. She had turned away from a tasteful display of ties, all beyond her means, when she saw Mr van Borsele walking down the arcade in her direction. He hadn't seen her, and no wonder: the fairylike creature from the car accident was tripping along beside him.

Claribel, driven by some strong feeling she didn't stop to analyse, opened the door of the exclusive men's shop whose window she had been looking at and hurried inside. She emerged ten minutes later, having purchased a tie with almost all the money in her purse, but nevertheless cheap at the price for it had enabled her to avoid Mr van Borsele.

She walked to Piccadilly Circus, turned down Haymarket and caught a bus to Stamford Street with the rest of the weekend looming emptily before her. It was providential that within half an hour of her return a junior surgical registrar at Jerome's should ring up to invite her to his birthday party.

'We're having it at the Dog and Thistle——' the pub frequented by the medical staff at Jerome's. 'Someone will fetch you and take you back. Miss Flute's coming, and Tilly and Pat——' both girls from the physio department. 'You know everyone.'

It turned out to be a pleasant, noisy evening: far too many people crammed into the private bar of the pub, eating potato crisps and drinking beer or tonic water; it was too near pay day for anything more expensive. It was almost eleven o'clock when Miss Flute edged her way over to where Claribel was at the centre of a group of several of the young doctors and signified her intention of going home.

'Pat's got the car here, she says she'll run us back if we'd like to go now.'

So Claribel eased her way to the door, calling goodbyes as she went, and got into Pat's elderly Austin with Miss Flute and presently was back in the flat, opening a can of soup, giving the cats a meal and getting ready for bed.

One of the more senior housemen had suggested that they might spend the next afternoon together and have tea. He was a serious young man, and she had been out with him once or twice; he was given to visiting museums and art galleries and they had enjoyed a casual acquaintance. She had said that she would go, for it would fill her day nicely. As he was on call after six o'clock, they had agreed to meet at two o'clock outside the National Gallery, so after a morning cleaning the flat and doing the chores, she got into a jersey dress, covered it with a raincoat since it was drizzling and caught a bus to Trafalgar Square, where she found him waiting for her.

He was a nice young man, undemanding, polite and able to talk well; they spent an hour or so in the National Gallery and then found a small café where they had tea. It was a pleasant afternoon and, back at the flat feeding the cats, she wondered why she hadn't enjoyed it more. Nicky was a serious, steady young man, her own age; she was aware that he liked her and that if she encouraged him he would more than like her. It was therefore surprising that she didn't really care if she never saw him again.

Miss Flute sent her to the wards on Monday morning. It would give her a chance to give Mr van Borsele a cool stare if he so much glanced at her, Claribel thought. It was a great pity that there was no sign of him; Mr Shutter took the round, remarking as they paused by a patient so that she might put him through his exercises, 'A pity Mr van Borsele had to return to Holland. He would have liked to see the results of his work here.'

Claribel murmured a reply. The feeling of disappointment she felt she put down to not having a chance to snub the man. She wasn't quite clear as to why she wished to do this; he had, after all, come and gone in her life and she would forget him completely—well, almost completely. He had made life interesting, even though they had argued each time they had met, and she had enjoyed his company.

The week seemed longer than usual. Several new patients came for treatment, a number of them very hard work, for they were naturally timid about exercising a painful arm or leg, and by Friday evening Claribel was tired and dispirited. The weekend loomed emptily before her. She could, of course, go home and as she got her supper she decided that she might do that, only it would have to be in the morning; she could go out early and do what shopping she had to do, and catch a late morning train; twenty-four hours at home might improve her mood. She decided against telling her mother, though; that could be left until the morning. Much cheered, she cleaned the flat, saw to Enoch and Toots, washed her hair, did her nails and went to bed.

She was out early. There were a few shops at the other end of Meadow Road; she bought what she needed and hurried back to pack a shoulder bag and put away her groceries, then telephone her mother.

The hearty thump on the door caused her to drop the bag of sugar she was emptying into her storage jar. Mr van Borsele was in Holland; Mr Shutter had told her so. A second thump sent her to the door which she prudently opened with the chain up.

'Hello,' said Mr van Borsele, at his most placid. 'I'm delighted to see that you have taken my advice at last. Now open the door, there's a good girl.'

Claribel peeped at him through the narrow opening. 'I'm just leaving,' she pointed out. 'So sorry, but I had no idea that you would be calling.'

'Well, of course you hadn't.' He looked down his nose at her. 'I shall stand here and thump the knocker until you let me in; there are curtains twitching already.'

She opened the door and he went past her into the living-room. 'I want to talk to you,' he observed, briskly businesslike. 'The most sensible thing seems for me to drive you down to Tisbury and we can talk on the way; in that way I shall have your full attention.'

He went into the kitchen and filled the kettle. 'Coffee?'

She followed him. 'Have you been in London all this time?'

He bent over the stove so that she didn't see the gleam in his eyes. 'No, in Holland. I crossed over last night.'

'So why have you come here?' She put two mugs on a tray and got the milk from the fridge.

He turned to look at her. 'We're still friends?'

She said huffily, 'I suppose so, although I don't see why . . .'

'Ah, you're still peevish,' he observed blandly. 'Did you buy anything in that shop with all the ties in the window?'

Claribel dropped the spoon she was holding. A slow blush crept up her face, contributing a delightful prettiness to her already very pretty face.

'You saw me! How mean can you get.'

He spooned instant coffee. 'Dear girl, mean because I didn't come into that shop and help you choose a tie? Or because I was with Irma Cooper?'

She said crossly, 'Is that her name?' then added icily, 'Not that I'm interested.'

'Why should you be?' He handed her a mug of coffee and smiled into her frowning face. 'I thought we might have luncheon on the way—the Old Drapery Stores again if you would like that? Go and do whatever you have to do while I stuff these cats into their basket.'

It was obvious to her that he had no intention of telling her anything until they were on their way. She tidied her hair and whisked herself into the new three-piece, reflecting as she did so that she spent a good deal of her free time making coffee and then being rushed to wherever Mr van Borsele desired to go. It would have to stop, but first she would find out what he wanted of her.

He was in no hurry to tell her; they talked trivialities as he drove westwards, falling into friendly silence from time to time, and even when they stopped for lunch at the Old Drapery Stores, he gave her no hint as to what he wished to discuss with her.

Claribel, a sensible girl, dismissed the matter for the more important one of enjoying her lunch: homemade soup, trout caught that morning and rhubarb tart which melted in the mouth, accompanied by a great dish of clotted cream. They drank tonic water since Mr van Borsele was driving and she had no wish to drink alone, and when they were having their coffee she ventured a question.

'This—whatever it is you want to talk about, what is it?'

'Presently.' He sounded remote and rather cold; for the life of her she felt unable to pursue the matter and was forced to contain her curiosity while he finished his coffee and presently ushered her back into the car.

Even then he said nothing. it wan't until they had turned off at Fovant and Tisbury was only a few miles away that he slid the Rolls to the side of the road and remarked, 'I want your attention, Claribel, and no interruptions.'

She said pertly, 'You sound as though you were going to deliver a lecture, but I'll listen—I can't do anything else, can I?'

She turned to look at him and saw that he was frowning. 'It's about that Irma, isn't it? Before you start, let me guess. You've fallen for her, but you've got a girl in Holland—perhaps you are engaged—and you don't know what to do. Though I should have thought you were the very last man to need help with anything.'

'Did I ever tell you that you have a splendid imagination Claribel? Yes, it is concerning Irma, and you are near enough the mark, but there is more to it than that. I left her at home in Bath and as far as I was concerned that was the end of it, but it seemed she wished to see me again. She discovered who I was and where I lived and worked. She has been a most unwelcome visitor ever since. I've treated her as I would treat any other woman of my acquaintance but she seems bent on plaguing me; I told her that I was going to be married but she refuses to believe me.' He turned to look at Claribel, and something in his face made her sit up straight. He went on, his voice silky, 'If I could produce a fiancée she would be convinced. It crossed my mind that you might consent to, er, take on that role in a temporary and nominal fashion . . .'

Her voice came out a squeak. 'Me? You must be mad! What about . . . I thought you were going to be married to a girl in Holland.'

'You may have thought that, but I believe I never actually told you so.' He smiled thinly. 'Your imagination again, Claribel.'

'Yes, well . . . It's ridiculous.'

'Of course it is. And trifling, but of course if you are going to magnify the whole matter out of all proportion then there is nothing more to be said.'

'What will you do?'

'Why, as to that, it's a simple matter for me to return to Holland. A pity, though, for Mr Shutter and I work well together and have several worthwhile projects we intended to set up.'

He spoke quietly, staring ahead of him, and Claribel, glancing at him, thought how grim his profile looked. She knew that his work was important to him and that he had done some splendid surgery at Jerome's; to have to give all that up because of some tiresome girl pestering him seemed unfair to him. She said, 'What exactly have you in mind?'

She watched his face as he turned towards her; one look of triumph at having got his way and she would refuse to help him. But there was no expression on his face at all, although he smiled at her.

'I'll explain and you can think about it over the weekend.

Irma is staying in London with friends. I haven't met them and I don't know where they live. She contrives to meet me when I get back in the evening and when I leave the flat in the morning; at times she has attached herself to me when I've been out—in the Burlington Arcade on one occasion; you saw that for yourself. She phones and leaves messages and is generally a nuisance. I rashly told her that I was engaged to be married but she refused to believe me. If I can produce a fiancée, however, it might discourage her . . .'

'Don't you know any other girls more suitable than I am?'

'I know any number of people in London, but if you think about it you must agree with me that you are exactly right—you are free in the evening and at the weekends, we can arrange to go out on the town without difficulty, you can come to my flat and I can go to yours.'

She said coldly, 'It all sounds very convenient for you.' She heaved an indignant breath; she was to be at his beck and call, was she? Her own social life was to be neglected to suit him. 'What about me?'

'It won't be for more than a week or so,' he told her soothingly. 'A few evenings out. Dinner and dancing or the theatre, places where we're likely to be seen by her or her friends—they haunt them at night, she told me; we are bound to meet them at one place or another. I'll drive you back with me in the evenings so that there is a good chance of her seeing you then.'

He fell into a placid silence and she said snappishly, 'You've got it all worked out, haven't you?'

He said blandly, 'But of course.'

'It would make a lovely plot for a romantic novel,' she snapped again.

He agreed in a voice which reminded her forcibly of a

grown-up pandering to a child's tantrums. 'Though I don't read them myself,' he added.

She had nothing to say to that but, after a few moments, 'The whole idea is ridiculous. I'm surprised at you for thinking it up in the first place.'

He laughed then. 'Well, let's get on, shall we?' he observed easily. 'Your people will be wondering why we are late.'

Most aggravatingly, he began to talk about the charms of the English countryside at that time of year, a subject which he maintained until they arrived at her home.

They were welcomed warmly and Claribel was surprised when Mr van Borsele accepted her mother's invitation to stay for tea. They had it in the sitting-room, around the fire, for the day had turned chilly. To the casual visitor the scene couldn't have been more convivial; the talk was general as Mrs Brown's sandwiches and cakes disappeared rapidly, and if Claribel was more silent than usual, no one remarked upon it. Mr van Borsele got up to go eventually and she reflected how quickly he had made himself at home with her parents as he bade them goodbye. At the door he told her, 'I'll collect you about six o'clock tomorrow, Claribel,' and gracefully refused Mrs Brown's invitation to have tea with them.

Watching the car's lights disappear, Mrs Brown said slowly, 'What a very nice man he is, and such beautiful manners.'

Her daughter eyed her stormily. 'Mother, when he wants something he is quite ruthless . . .'

'Well, dear, I suppose a clever man such as he, performing small miracles of surgery almost every day of his life, is entitled to have his own way sometimes.'

'Always, Mother, always.'

'Such a pity you don't like him,' murmured Mrs Brown. She stole a look at her daughter's cross face. 'That friend of Sebastian's is staying at the refectory; he was wondering if you would be at home this weekend. How about giving him a ring?'

'Him? Malcolm something or other? He's so young, Mother!'

An answer which pleased her parent mightily.

CHAPTER SIX

THERE wasn't much of Saturday left, and although Claribel would have liked to confide in her mother she could see the good sense of saying nothing. Mr van Borsele could change his mind. Besides, if he went back to Holland within a day or so, there would surely be no need for his hare-brained scheme to be put into action. She spent the evening sitting cosily by the fire with Rover and the cats at her feet, listening to her mother's gentle gossip about the village and giving in her turn a faithful account of her week at Jerome's, although she had little to say about Mr van Borsele. To her mother's carefully casual enquiries she replied airily that he had returned unexpectedly from Holland and she had no idea how long he would be in England.

Sunday, comfortably filled by walking Rover, going to church, passing the time of day with various friends at the church door and going home to Sunday lunch, flew by too fast. She had stuffed her bag with her overnight things and one of her mother's mouthwatering fruit cakes, and was sitting round the fire eating buttery muffins, when Mr van Borsele arrived.

He apologised for being early and, at her mother's invitation, sat down beside her father's chair and started on the muffins, falling into easy conversation with Mr Brown. He had left his sister's home rather earlier than he had intended, he explained, and he hoped that he wasn't putting Claribel out in any way.

As though he hadn't put her out enough, she thought indignantly and told him in a cool voice that half an hour or so made no difference to her. She went on to remark about the rather chilly weather. 'It probably spoilt your weekend,' she observed and got up to pour second cups.

'There are so many things other than weather which can spoil a weekend,' he remarked blandly, 'just as it can turn out completely successful when it is least expected to.'

She eyed him uncertainly, wondering if he was referring to his scheme, and met his bland stare. 'One lump or two?' she asked him, so sharply that her mother looked at her in surprise.

He seemed in no hurry to go. Her mother's cake, a Victoria sponge, and a slice of gingerbread were sampled in turn with enjoyment and a well-phrased compliment or two which delighted her mother. When they finally left it was well past six o'clock.

It was frustrating of him to remain silent for long stretches of time and when he did speak it was on some trivial topic. They were on the motorway, rapidly approaching London, before he asked, 'Are you doing anything this evening? I thought we might have dinner somewhere?'

'The cats,' she reminded him, aware of pleasure warming her chilly thoughts.

'Shall we go to the flat first? You can feed them or whatever and we can go on from there.'

She agreed readily enough; to dine out would make a pleasant end to a weekend which hadn't been altogether pleasant. She debated with herself as to whether she should bring up the subject of his scheme and decided not to say anything about it. She had more or less refused to have anything to do with it and he hadn't pressed her for an answer. It was a pity if the girl was being a nuisance, but surely he could think of something . . .

At the flat she saw to the cats, did her face and her hair and pronounced herself ready. 'There's no need to dress up, is there?' she asked anxiously.

'None at all; you look very nice in that thing.'

The kind of remark Sebastian might make. She got into the car and tried not to smile when Mr van Borsele gravely saluted the inquisitive face peering from the next door window.

He drove to the Savoy. It was only as she got out of the car that she was struck by an unpleasant thought. 'Is this one of the places Irma comes to?'

He nodded to the doorman to get the car parked before taking her arm and marching her through the imposing doors. 'Yes. Shall we have a drink first?'

She said softly in a fierce voice, 'No, I'd like to go back to my flat, now.' She gave him a look to wither him up completely, only it didn't appear to make any difference to him. 'You planned this, didn't you? I told you it was a silly idea . . .'

'The word was ridiculous. I was so sure that you would have second thoughts, Claribel, and agree to help me. You're a sensible girl, there's no romantic nonsense about you, and after all it is such a trifling little matter for you.'

They had paused on the way to the bar and she gave him a long deliberate look. His opinion of her was galling to say the least.

'I don't really see why I should allow you to make use of

me just to get you out of a hole.'

He had never looked more patiently reasonable. He said gently, 'You're just about the nicest person I know, Claribel, and certainly the most beautiful. Irma will take one good look at you and know that she hasn't got a chance.'

She went faintly pink, 'You have no need to say that. Anyway, she's seen me already.'

'That's why you're so exactly right.' He smiled. It was a charming smile, warm and reassuring; she reflected idiotically that if she was one of his patients and he had just told her that he was going to amputate an arm or a leg she would accept the horrid news with complete trust.

'All right. But just as soon as she leaves you alone or goes home it's to stop.'

He raised his eyebrows. 'But of course, Claribel.' He dug a hand into a pocket and put something into her hand. A diamond ring, three large stones surrounded by circles of smaller stones. She opened her mouth to protest but his hand closed over hers. 'Put it on . . .'

'It's not real?' she half whispered.

'Of course it's real. It belonged to my great-grandmother. Shall we have that drink?'

They went into the bar and she tried not to gape at the magnificent jewels on her finger while she drank her sherry, an excellent one which as far as she was concerned could have been tap water. They went into the Grill Room presently and she felt disquiet at their table: in a prominent position in the centre of the room.

'Just right,' murmured Mr van Borsele. 'Put your hand on the table and flash the ring; Irma is sitting quite close by with a party of people.'

She had the good sense not to look around her and buried

her pretty nose in the menu while she steadied her breath. Mr van Borsele's calm voice was suggesting that caviare might be good to start with, and how did she like the idea of chicken *à la* king?'

They had ordered and he was telling the wine waiter to bring a bottle of champagne when Irma arrived at the table. Claribel, mindful of her companion's wishes, laid a hand on the cloth so that the ring was in full view, arranged her features into an expression of friendly surprise and watched Mr van Borsele get to his feet.

Irma spoke before anyone else had a chance. 'Where have you been?' she demanded. 'I haven't seen you for ages. You must know . . .' Her eyes caught the sparkle of the diamonds on Claribel's hand and she stopped.

Claribel returned her glare with a sweet smile. 'Hello,' she said with every appearance of pleasure. 'Do you remember me? When you had that accident—we took you to my home before Marc drove you to Bath.'

She turned a dazzling smile upon Mr van Borsele. 'We've often talked about it, haven't we, darling?'

'You are engaged?' Irma looked at them in turn. 'So it's true. I didn't believe you, but it's true.' Her eyes fastened on the ring. 'Not that it's important; engagements don't mean much these days.' She tossed her head and smiled at Mr van Borsele, who smiled back thinly.

'Ours does,' he told her. 'Now if you would excuse us, we have a great deal to discuss—plans for the wedding and so on.' He glanced over to the table she had left. 'I think your friends are waiting to leave.'

Irma left without a word and presently departed with her companions without looking at them again. Claribel, spreading caviare on toast with a hand which shook very slightly, couldn't quite suppress a sigh of relief.

'Women,' observed Mr van Borsele, 'never fail to surprise me. Just for a few minutes I actually believed that you and I were engaged.' He smiled at her in what she considered to be a smug fashion. 'You should call me "darling" more often; it does something to my ego.'

She choked on a morsel of toast. 'Your ego doesn't need any propping up. You're Mr van Borsele, and Mr van Borsele you'll remain, as far as I'm concerned.'

'Marc?' he suggested. 'We're bound to meet the tiresome girl again and you might slip up.'

'I should imagine you're rid of her after that little scene.' She studied the chicken *à la* king which has just been set before her; her appetite had in no way been impaired by her acting. 'How fortunate that we should meet her so soon; we can call the whole thing off.'

'Certainly not; she's badly adjusted mentally, and spoilt and selfish and uninhibited; it will take more than one encounter with us as a devoted engaged couple to convince her.'

'Oh, will it? Aren't you going back to Holland?'

'What I like about you, Claribel, is your plain speaking. I am aware that you have a poor opinion of me, but I beg that you will endeavour to overcome that until I can, as it were, sink without trace.'

She remained unmoved. 'So you're not going back to Holland?'

'For the moment, no. Mr Shutter and I are joining forces over a child who sadly needs extensive surgery; we hope to get to work on her next week. Which means that you and I will be free to show ourselves as a loving couple on several evenings.'

'Which evenings?' she wanted to know. 'I have plans as well.' Her glass had been filled for a second time and she took a defiant sip of champagne.

'It's hard to say at the moment. I expect I shall be at the hospital until quite late tomorrow evening; I'll call in on my way home and let you know if Tuesday evening will be free. So if you have a date for tomorrow evening, go ahead.' He spoke in a kindly voice which annoyed her very much. 'Only don't go anywhere you are likely to be seen by Irma.'

She said coldly and crossly, 'How am I to know where she will be? Anyway, I never go out on a Monday evening; I wash my hair.'

'I'll dry it for you while we make our plans.' And, at her outraged look, 'Quite permissible by Meadow Road standards. After all, we are engaged.' He smiled his sudden beguiling smile. 'Now, shall we bury the hatchet and enjoy ourselves?'

Which, surprisingly, she did.

Monday was always a busy day and she got home rather later than usual. She got her supper, fed Enoch and Toots, washed the smalls, prudently set the coffee tray ready and washed her hair. It was almost ten o'clock and she was sitting in her dressing-gown drying it when the door knocker resounded with the familiar thump. She unlocked the door, leaving the chain up, and Mr van Borsele said, 'Good girl. Open up.'

She stood aside as he went in and followed him into the living-room.

'It's rather late,' observed Claribel.

'Not so late that the neighbours aren't peering at me through their curtains.' He stood looking at her. Her abundant hair hung in a golden stream down her back, not quite dry. 'Come and sit on this stool and I'll finish that for you.'

There seemed nothing strange in sitting down at his feet while he settled in the armchair, took a towel from her and began a vigourous rubbing.

'Had a busy day?' she asked through a tangle of hair.

'Very, but I think we've got it right. If it all goes as it should we'll be able to lengthen her legs by six inches; she'll still be on the short side when she has grown, but at least she won't be grotesque.'

'Oh—is it that operation where someone has to turn a key each day?'

'Well, something like that, yes. Daily manipulation enables the bone to lengthen gradually. We've dealt with one leg; if it's a success we'll do the other in due course.' He took up a length of her hair and began on it. 'What a mass of hair you have, Claribel. They should have called you Rapunzel.'

'I've been wondering if I should have it cut.'

'Don't you dare. You'll probably get the child for physio. Have you been busy today?'

'Not nearly as busy as you. Are you going back to Jerome's?'

'Yes, but if it goes as it should I thought you and I might have an evening out tomorrow. Remind me to give you the ring again.'

She mumbled behind her hair. She had given it back on the previous evening, growing shy and awkward doing it—stupidly, as he had taken it from her in a matter-of-fact way. She tossed her hair out of her eyes and took the towel from him. 'Thanks; that's dry enough to plait. Would you like a cup of coffee before you go?'

'I've only just got here,' he complained mildly, 'but, yes, I'd like that.'

She made coffee for them both and they drank it in a companionable silence before he got to his feet.

'Tomorrow then,' he said. 'Now, let me see—you'd better dine at my place and we can go on from there. A bit dressy, I think. I'll call for you at seven o'clock unless you get a message to the contrary.'

To all of which she agreed meekly enough. She had agreed to help him; in for a penny in for a pound. And there was no denying that he was a delightful companion with whom to spend an evening, even if they did argue most of the time. She saw him to the door and wished him goodnight, and was quite unprepared for his kiss.

The following morning Miss Flute told her that she would be treating the little girl Mr van Borsele and Mr Shutter had operated on. 'She is still in intensive care. You're to give her breathing exercises for the first few days, ten-minute sessions, TDS. She'll be going to Crispin Ward once she is fit enough. They want you at ten o'clock.'

The intensive care unit was on the top floor of the hospital, next door to the theatre block, a daunting place to the layman, full of technical apparatus, yards of tubing and computer screens, and manned by teams of nurses round the clock. There were several patients there, but the little girl was the one Claribel had to deal with. The child was small, with a white face and enormous dark eyes.

Claribel knelt down by the bed. 'Hello, poppet. I've come to help get you well again. We're going to play some breathing games; I'm sure you'll win every time.' She talked to the child for a little while and then pulled up a chair and began the exercises which had been ordered, going cautiously. Each day they would be stepped up but just at first she had to gain the little girl's confidence. Ten minutes wasn't long; they parted the best of friends. Claribel slipped quietly away and started for the stairs. Half-way down she met Mr van Borsele going up. He stopped by her.

'Ah, good morning, Miss Brown. You've been with Rita?'

Her cool, 'Good morning, Mr van Borsele,' was uttered in her best profesional manner and the corners of his mouth twitched. 'Rita has been very good, although she is apprehensive. I think we'll have to keep to the simple breathing exercises for a couple of days until I have her complete confidence.'

He nodded. 'Good, good. I'll leave that to your capable judgement.'

With a nod he had gone on his way, leaving her vaguely annoyed, although she wasn't sure why.

She was kept busy for the rest of the day with a snatched sandwich lunch and a cup of tea gulped down during the afternoon. As she dressed that evening she thought about her dinner—a substantial one, she hoped; she was famished.

She had chosen to wear a long-skirted dress of green crêpe which exactly matched her eyes. It was discreetly simple in cut, elegant and severely plain, suitable she hoped for whatever evening Mr van Borsele had in mind; he had, after all, told her to wear something dressy. She put on her very best slippers—bronze kid with very high heels, a wicked extravagance she had been unable to resist—and from the depths of her wardrobe hauled out a mohair wrap, a long-ago gift to her mother who had handed it over to Claribel, quite rightly observing that such a garment could only be seen to advantage on a tall, queenly figure. Claribel had accepted it with delight, telling her indignant parent that it was just the thing to cover her buxom person.

'You are not buxom,' Mrs Brown had declared, 'and you never will be. You work too hard.'

'I might marry,' Claribel had said flippantly, 'and live a life of sloth.'

Her mother had snorted indignantly. 'If you marry, love, a husband and children won't give you any chance to idle.'

Mr van Borsele was punctual, but then he always was. He had been home first, that was apparent as soon as she cast eyes on the elegance of his attire. He looked more handsome than ever in a dinner-jacket; no wonder the tiresome Irma found him irresistible.

She said, 'Hello, or should I say good evening, Mr van Borsele?'

He came to stand in front of her. 'Don't be pert; there is a time and a place for everything. You look charming.' He bent and kissed her, adding, 'If you see what I mean.'

He picked up the wrap. 'Must we cover your charms?' he wanted to know, and Claribel, for once feeling shy, said, 'Well, it is chilly in the evening,' and swathed the garment around her.

'We'll have to go via Jerome's,' he told her as they went out to the car. 'I want to check on Rita.'

'She's not so well?' Claribel turned a concerned face to him.

'She's splendid, but Shutter's out of town and I want a word with Night Sister about her.'

Sitting in the car, waiting for him, Claribel thought idly that being married to a doctor or a surgeon was, to say the least, a life of unexpected happenings: late meals, no meals at all, broken nights, difficult patients, and, in the case of an eminent surgeon such as Marc, a good deal of travelling. As he got back into the car she asked, 'Is everything going well?'

'It's early days, my dear, but I'm hoping so. Another day or two and we'll feel more certain of it.'

'Have you done this particular operation before?'

He was going over Westminster Bridge, and the overhead lights showed his rather stern profile. 'Half a dozen times.'

'And all successful?'

'Yes, to date.'

She said in a worried way, 'You know, I think I'm a bit in awe of you—you're clever, and you do things that few other people would dare to do.'

He laughed. 'If I were asked to cut out and make one of your dresses I wouldn't have the faintest idea where to start. Perhaps others don't dare to pick up a scalpel, but *I* don't dare to let myself pick up dressmaking scissors.'

He gave her a quick glance. 'What is it you say in English? "It takes all sorts to make a world".' He drove along Whitehall and turned into Trafalgar Square, into Pall Mall and then began to work his way through the one-way streets until they were in Wigmore Street where soon he turned into one of the quiet streets close by and stopped before a terrace of Regency houses, with handsome porches and well-tended window-boxes. There was only the muted sound of traffic and there were trees lining the pavement.

'Very nice,' said Claribel, taking it all in as she got out of the car.

He had her arm. 'London can be delightful,' he observed, 'and it is convenient for the rooms I share with Shutter.'

They were mounting the three steps which led to the

front door and he took out his keys. 'Oh, do you have private patients as well?' She answered herself. 'Of course you do.'

'Well, yes.' He opened the door and ushered her into a vestibule opening on to a fair-sized hall. A porter was standing there who bade them good evening and went towards a lift to open its gates. Mr van Borsele flapped a large hand. 'We'll walk thanks, George—healthy exercise.'

They went unhurriedly up the stairs to the next floor and he opened one of the doors on the carpeted landing. The lobby they entered was square with a number of doors leading from it. Mr van Borsele took her wrap and threw it over an English elbow-chair, calling at the same time, 'Tilly, come and meet Miss Brown.'

Tilly was small and round and brisk with grey hair and twinkly blue eyes; she bounced into the lobby almost before he had finished speaking and fetched up in front of Claribel.

'Claribel, this is Tilly, my housekeeper and old friend; she cooks like a dream, rules the cleaning lady with a rod of iron and keeps a firm hand on me.'

The housekeeper grinned at him as Claribel said, 'How do you do' and shook hands. 'Don't you believe a word, miss,' observed Tilly. ''Is lordship does just what 'e wants, bless 'is 'eart.' She eyed Claribel. 'You're as pretty as a peach—all that lovely 'air. A sight better than that nasty little piece 'oo comes poking her nose in where she's not wanted.'

She whisked away again, saying as she went, 'You can 'ave ten minutes, then I'll dish up.'

Mr van Borsele hadn't said a word; he pushed open a door and stood aside for Claribel to go into the room beyond: a charming room, high ceilinged with a bow window at one end. The walls were panelled and it was furnished most comfortably with armchairs and with a large sofa on either side of the fireplace. Small wine tables, some with lighted lamps, were scattered around, and a mahogany break-front bookcase with glass doors stood against one wall. There were flowers, too, and some charming pieces of china; a beautiful room, she decided, admiring the brocade curtains at the window.

'Do sit down,' advised Mr van Borsele. 'We have time for a drink before Tilly dishes up.'

Claribel was still getting over her surprise; she hadn't expected such a lovely home and certainly she had been taken aback by Tilly and her down-to-earth Cockney manner. Mr van Borsele handed her a glass and said thoughtfully, 'You are surprised . . .' He was interrupted by the telephone on the table at his elbow. He lifted the receiver, listened for a moment without speaking and then beckoned Claribel and handed it to her. Mystified, she took it from him silently. It was Irma.

'Who is that?' she demanded.

'Claribel Brown,' said Claribel in her sweetest voice. 'Can I help you?'

'I want to speak to Marc.'

'I'm afraid he is in the shower,' said Claribel. 'Can I give him a message?'

'I might have known you'd be there,' said the sharp voice into her ear. 'Are you really going to marry him?'

'Oh, yes. We're deciding the date this evening.'

'It's so sudden,' said Irma suspiciously.

'Love at first sight, you know,' said Claribel in what she hoped was a convincing voice. 'I must go,' she finished naughtily, 'I haven't finished dressing!'

She put down the receiver and looked across at Mr van Borsele, who was watching her with a thoughtful expression. 'I could hardly believe my ears! If I didn't know you better I would have believed every word you uttered.'

She had the grace to blush. 'Well, I had to say something on the spur of the moment.'

'I would be interested to hear what you might tell her if you had the time to consider . . .'

She took a heartening sip of sherry. 'Well, you really are too bad. There was no earthly reason why I should be made to answer the phone.'

'My apologies, Claribel, but you must admit that it was effective.'

He smiled so disarmingly that she found herself smiling too.

Tilly was a splendid cook. They dined in an atmosphere of cordiality, doing justice to her watercress soup, Dover sole and rhubarb pie and cream. Over coffee they decided where they should go next.

'Now, where do you suppose a newly engaged couple, very much in love, would go?' asked Mr van Borsele.

She considered. 'Somewhere to dance.'

'The London Hilton. Not quite my choice, but sooner or later I believe that one meets everyone there.' He fished in a pocket and gave her the ring. 'Put that on, there's a good girl.' He raised his voice. 'Tilly, show Miss Brown where she can tidy herself.'

Claribel was beginning to enjoy herself; she had no idea that Marc could be such fun. It surprised her, on thinking about it, that she had ever disliked him or thought him cold and reserved. Of course, she mused as she did her face in the splendidly equipped cloakroom, once she had fulfilled her role of fiancée and Irma had been dispatched for good, he might possibly revert to his old manner, but in the meantime it was a nice change from her little flat.

The Hilton was crowded but they were given a good table. Mr van Borsele ordered champagne, but they didn't drink it at once, taking instead to the dance floor. They danced well, the pair of them, not talking until he said softly to the top of her head, 'The gods are with us; Irma is here, sitting at a table with half a dozen others. Could you look up at me in an adoring manner when I give you a dig?'

She gave a little splutter of laughter and then, at a sharp poke in the ribs, smiled up at him. She was quite unprepared for the look on his face; tender and loving and somehow exciting. It was gone almost as soon as she saw it. When she looked again he was looking over her head, his features austere; she must have imagined it, she thought uneasily.

They went back to their table presently and he said, 'About tomorrow: I've seats for the theatre—*Starlight Express*. We'll dine at the Connaught first. And on Friday we'll drive out of town. I must be at Jerome's on Thursday evening so I'll come round to your place. Saturday I'll get a table at the Ritz; we can dance there.'

'And when do I get the chance to wash my hair?' added Claribel with a slight edge to her voice. 'Or for that matter have a few hours to myself?'

'On Sunday, I'll fetch you about ten o'clock and take you to Tisbury.'

'And supposing I don't wish to go?'

'Don't be silly. You can sit and drowse in your father's delightful garden and mull over the week. I'll pick you up at about seven o'clock.'

'What happens when people don't want to do what you have planned?'

He gave her a bland look. 'But, my dear, they do, and if by any chance they don't, I persuade them.'

She said slowly, 'You know, when I first met you . . .'

'You didn't like me!' he finished for her. 'You're still not sure, are you?' He gave her a little mocking smile. 'Shall we dance again?'

Presently he took her home, refusing nicely enough to go in and bidding her a cheerful goodnight without any reference to the evening they had spent together.

Of course she saw him the next morning for she had to go to the intensive care unit to start little Rita on her exercises, but beyond a civil good morning they didn't speak and when she returned at midday and later again in the afternoon, he was operating. It was Miss Flute who gave her his message.

'You're to be ready for six-forty-five,' she told Claribel. She looked as though she wanted to ask questions but she didn't.

It was Claribel who said, 'It's all right, Miss Flute, I'm helping Mr van Borsele with a small problem, that's all.'

Miss Flute eyed the pretty face smiling so nicely at her. She was fond of Claribel, who worked hard and didn't grumble, and she cherished a secret passion for Mr van Borsele; she had been hoping that she was taking a small part in a romance between them, but neither of them had evinced the least sign of it. She sighed and reminded Claribel that Mrs Snow was waiting.

Luckily it was a day when the physio department finished its work on time. Claribel, home in good time, spent ten minutes or so deciding what she was going to wear. A short dress, she decided, dark blue crêpe-de-Chine, pleated from a yoke, with long tight sleeves and an important belt which emphasised her slim waist. It was especially good as a background for her golden hair and green eyes and proved to be exactly right for the evening. In bed, hours later, she thought with satisfaction of Mr van Borsele's quick look of approval. The evening had been a success, too. She had never been to the Connaught before; its quiet elegance had pleased her and, besides, Mr van Borsele had put himself out to be an interesting companion. Best of all, *Starlight Express* had been better than she had expected. A heavenly few hours, she had to admit, and then fell to wondering if he expected supper on the following evening. He had warned her that he might be late—after seven o'clock. Sandwiches, she decided drowsily, or, if she had time, sausage rolls. Or had she better cook a hot meal? She slept on the problem.

They saw nothing of each other the next day. Mr van Borsele was in theatre for hours on end and there was no sign of him when she went to put little Rita through her exercises. Back at the flat she made tea for herself, saw to Enoch and Toots, made a batch of sausage rolls and, after a little thought, another batch, this time of apple turnovers.

By seven o'clock she had the table set with plates and coffee mugs, a bowl of fruit and the apple turnovers; the sausage rolls were keeping hot in the oven. By eight o'clock she was getting restless; she was also getting hungry. About then she ate a sausage roll and sat down to read, only to give that up presently to ponder if he was coming after all. Presumably not, she decided, as the clock struck nine. In ten minutes, she promised herself she would have her own supper, lock the door and get ready for bed.

She was actually on the way to the kitchen when the door suffered its usual hefty thump. She went to let him in, prudently leaving the chain up and taking her time about undoing it. But she was sorry about that when she saw his face. He was tired, weary to his bones, and somehow it was all the more obvious because he was his usual immaculate self. The kind of man, she reflected, who would shave in the middle of the Sahara.

She answered his terse, 'I'm late,' with a soothing murmur.

'Coffee first?' she asked and drew the armchair nearer the gas fire. She handed him his coffee and sat down quietly opposite him. Only when he had drunk almost all the coffee did she ask, 'A bad day? Not little Rita, I hope?'

'She's fine. And nothing went wrong; it was a long list . . .'

'That girl with the fractured pelvis?'

He told her about it and she listened quietly. Finally he said, 'What a good listener you are, Claribel.'

'I'm interested. When did you last eat?'

'I had a sandwich around lunchtime.'

She fed him the sausage rolls and then the apple turnovers washed down with more coffee, and when he had finished she said, 'Now you must go home and go to bed. Have you a list in the morning?'

'No, only rounds and Out-patients at two o'clock.' He smiled a little. 'You sound like my old nanny. Shall we go somewhere quiet tomorrow evening? Shutter will be taking over for twenty-hour hours so I should be free by six o'clock. I'll come straight here from Jerome's and you can come back to the flat with me; we'll go from there.'

It was remarkable what food and drink had done for him;

he looked quite his old self again. She agreed willingly enough. 'No dressing up?' she wanted to know.

He shook his head. 'We'll find a restaurant somewhere and eat whatever they've got.' He stood up and stretched hugely. 'Thank you, Claribel, you're a good girl.' He bent and kissed her cheek lightly. 'Goodnight.'

When he had gone she tidied away the plates and mugs, ate another sausage roll and went finally to bed, with the cats lying comfortably on her feet. They weren't supposed to do that but somehow she was glad of their company.

She was in the physio department all the next day except for her short spells with Rita. Mrs Green went to Outpatients in the afternoon and Claribel was kept busy until it was time to go home. Once there, she saw to the cats, put everything ready for the morning, showered and changed into a jacket and a skirt with a plain silk blouse, did her face with care, patted her golden hair to pristine tidiness and sat down to wait.

Not for long; it was barely six o'clock as she got into the car. Traffic was heavy and it took longer than usual to reach Mr van Borsele's flat. As he drew up before the door Claribel said sharply, 'That's Irma—coming down the steps.'

He thrust his hand into a pocket and gave her the ring, opened her door and got out himself to come round and take her arm as she got out, too.

'Remember that you love me to distraction,' he said softly as they crossed the pavement.

Irma stood watching them. Mr van Borsele greeted her without any sign of embarrassment and after a moment Claribel said, 'Hello, Irma. Did you want to see us?'

Irma said nothing but flung away to where an MG sports

car stood. She got in and drove off without a word.

'Do you suppose she is tiring?' asked Claribel with interest.

'Let us hope so. Come in; you can have a drink while I change.'

Tilly welcomed her with a beaming smile as he settled her in an easy chair in the sitting-room, poured her a drink and disappeared, to reappear very shortly with a brisk, 'Well, are you ready?'

For all the world as though I had been the one who had kept him waiting, thought Claribel with a touch of peevishness.

The peevishness disappeared, though, as they drove out of London. He took her to the Waterside at Bray, elegant and charming and overlooking the river, and even on a rather chilly summer evening, it was a delight to have drinks and watch the countryside. They dined presently: a pâté of fish followed by duck with stuffed vegetables and, to finish, lemon tart for her while Mr van Borsele contented himself with the cheeseboard. They lingered over coffee and Claribel allowed a feeling of well-being to sweep over her; life, after all, was really rather nice and her companion was rather nice, too. She rose reluctantly when he suggested that they had better return. 'I've a list as long as an arm tomorrow,' he observed. 'I want to get as much done before I go back.'

'Go back?' She was startled. 'Are you going back to Holland?'

'Well, yes. I only come here from time to time, you know . . .'

She did know; he specialised in several techniques which meant that he was in demand in countries other than his own. All the same, she said, 'So you don't need to bother about Irma once you've gone back home.'

They were in the car now, already on the motorway on the way to London.

'I'm not sure about that. She's bored and spoilt and has nothing better to do than follow her own inclinations. If she feels like it she could follow me wherever I choose to go. And I'm sorry if that sounds conceited. My hope is that she will set eyes on some other man and develop a fancy for him.'

He threw her a sideways look. 'Claribel, when I go back to Holland I should like you to come with me.'

She gaped at him. 'Me? Go with you? Whatever for?'

'It would, I think, clinch the matter. You can stay with my grandmother.'

'I don't know your grandmother,' snapped Claribel, much put out, 'and I refuse, so please don't mention it again.'

He said silkily, 'I imagined that would be your reaction, but just let the idea simmer, will you?'

'It's impossible. I've no holiday due, and what about Enoch and Toots?'

He didn't answer, which was most unsatisfactory. Nor would he come in when they reached her flat. He saw her to the door, reminded her that they were to go dancing on the following evening, held out his hand for the ring and drove away, apparently quite unconcerned at her refusal.

CHAPTER SEVEN

CLARIBEL spent a good deal of the night worrying away at Mr van Borsele's strange request. Well, it hadn't really been a request, rather a statement of something which he had taken for granted. And for once he had gone too far. All he was thinking of was his own convenience. And if his grandmother was half as bossy as he was, the visit would be nothing less than sheer misery. She lay picturing herself sitting between the pair of them, two haughty noses and two pairs of dark eyes boring into her, organising her days to suit themselves . . . And more than likely Granny wouldn't speak a word of English; she had no intention of letting the ridiculous idea simmer.

She spent Saturday shopping and cleaning her little home and composing cool, logical speeches to make to Mr van Borsele when he came. It was a great pity that when he did, he gave her no opportunity to say a word about it. His talk was of ordinary things as he whisked her off to the Ritz to dine and dance until the small hours. After a brief period of deciding coolness on her part, he wanted to know if she was sulking about something. 'And if you are, you are to stop it at once, for Irma has just come in.'

They were sitting at a table which had a splendid view of the restaurant, and where they could be seen. She had promised to play a part for him and she was an honest girl; she gave him a dazzling smile just in time. Irma was

127

passing their table and stopped.

She said sulkily, 'Together again? Have you moved in with him, then?'

A faint pink covered Claribel's cheeks. 'Oh, hello, Irma.' Her voice was sugary-sweet and Mr van Borsele's mouth quivered ever so slightly.

'Well, no, I'd love to but I work at a hospital, you know; it would take me too long to get to and fro each day. But that won't be for much longer . . .'

Mr van Borsele's voice was very smooth. 'I shall be going back shortly and of course Claribel will go with me.' The bland expression didn't alter when Claribel gave him a sharp kick under the table; on the shin and painful. She was still smiling but only for Irma's benefit.

'Back to Holland?' asked Irma.

Mr van Borsele gave her a look of well-bred surprise. 'Naturally. That is my home.'

'Whereabouts?'

Claribel chipped in, 'How long are you staying in London?' Her smile was wide; there was nothing in her quiet voice to suggest the violence she would like to do to the wretched girl.

'What you mean is,' said Irma rudely, 'that there is no point in me trying to get Marc away from you.'

'Something like that,' agreed Claribel. She turned her green eyes upon him. 'Darling, could we order? I'm famished.'

She suspected that behind his impassive politeness he was amused, but his, 'Of course, dearest. I'm sure Irma will excuse us,' couldn't be faulted.

Irma flounced away to her own table. He sat down again and, just in case she should turn round to look at them, took Claribel's ringed hand in his. 'You would be a splendid receptionist for a busy man,' he observed. 'Would you consider giving up your job and coming to work for me?'

'Certainly not,' Claribel spoke a shade tartly. 'And anyway, I've not got the slightest idea how to be a receptionist.'

'It's a gift one is born with: the ability to tell whopping great fibs with the voice of a dove and to smile like an angel at the same time.' He added blandly, 'I'd pay you handsomely.'

She withdrew her hand from his and studied the menu she had been handed. 'For two pins I'd get up and go back to the flat.'

'By all means, but do eat something first. What about *duo de langoustines*, and ragout of salmon and scallops to follow, and I think champagne, don't you? After all, we have something to celebrate.'

'What?' asked Claribel. Her thoughts were on the delicious dinner suggested to her and she had forgotten to be tart.

'The future,' said Mr van Borsele at his blandest.

That sounded harmless enough; she settled down to enjoy her dinner. It was every bit as good as it had sounded, and the iced curacao mousse with strawberries, which followed the scallops and salmon served with watercress sauce, mushrooms and truffles, left her in a pleasant state of repletion which, however, didn't prevent her getting up to dance at his suggestion with every sign of pleasure.

Just before she went to sleep that night she thought drowsily that Marc van Borsele certainly knew how to take a girl out in style. She smacked her lips at the memory of the mousse and went happily to sleep.

On their way to Tisbury the following morning she asked him rather diffidently if he would like to lunch at her home, but he declined with reluctance; she was told his sister was expecting him and, since she wouldn't be seeing him for some time, he had promised to spend the day with her and her husband and the baby, adding that he intended leaving towards the end of the week.

'And you are still adamant in refusing to come with me?' he asked.

'Well, of course I am. I can't leave my job at a moment's notice.'

'In that case, give in your notice tomorrow and I'll come over for you.'

She turned in her seat to look at him. 'Just for once,' she told him severely, 'you're not going to have your own way. I've helped you because I said I would, but that's the lot.'

He said mildly, 'You could take your holidays; I'm sure dear Miss Flute could contrive to let you go—family affairs, or something like that.'

She said stubbornly, 'It's no use; it's a good job and I have to work.'

It was very disconcerting when he agreed cheerfully and suggested that they should stop for coffee.

He didn't say another word about his suggestion, but spent ten minutes talking to her mother and father, warned her to be ready by seven o'clock that evening and drove away, leaving her feeling dreary and deprived, but of what she had no idea.

That Claribel was *distraite* was obvious to Mrs Brown but she didn't remark upon it; her beautiful daughter was up to something or other, and Mrs Brown hoped fervently that the something was to do with Marc van Borsele. It was most fortunate that Sebastian was coming home for the day: the brother and sister were close and she might unburden herself to him.

But she didn't. She was delighted to see him, they exchanged outrageous stories, teased each other and argued amicably, but somehow Mr van Borsele wasn't mentioned. Not until the afternoon as they sat at tea did Claribel let fall the information that she was being given a lift by someone from the hospital.

'Who?' asked Sebastian. 'Some callow medical student?'

'Well I dare say he was years ago, although it's hard to think of him as such. He's one of the consultants; divides his time between Jerome's and some hospital or other in Holland.'

Sebastian sat up. 'He's not by any chance called van Borsele?'

'Yes. Why?'

'Only, my dear sister, you've hooked one of the cleverest and most famous orthopaedic men there is around. I say, is he coming here?'

'Well, of course. Why all the fuss? He's got a bad temper and he likes his own way.'

'Don't we all? He's a real workaholic, too.'

'He dances very nicely,' observed Claribel demurely.

To all of which conversation her mother listened with the greatest satisfaction.

Mr van Borsele arrived punctually, accepting a mug of coffee from Mrs Brown, shook hands with Mr Brown and Sebastian and nodded casually to Claribel. There was nothing loverlike about the nod, nor did Claribel evince any sign of delight at the sight of him; Mrs Brown was quite put out. She felt better after they had gone, though; Sebastian, sitting on the kitchen table while she got the supper, remarked idly, 'So our old Clari has succumbed at last.'

Mrs Brown stopped beating eggs to look at him. 'What do you mean, dear?'

'Why, Mother, it's as plain as the nose on my face; they're in love.'

Mrs Brown brightened visibly. 'You really think so? But he hardly speaks to her when she is fetched and Claribel is quite offhand.'

'Clari hasn't discovered it yet and he's far too clever to do anything about it.' He helped himself to a slice of bread from the loaf on the table. 'You mark my words, Mother dear, we've got a romance on our hands.'

There was nothing romantic about Mr van Borsele's manner as they drove back to London. He talked intermittently about nothing much, and as for Claribel, she said hardly a word. She had given the matter a good deal of thought and was feeling, surprisingly enough, mean. Mr van Borsele had treated her generously, even if for his own ends, and she had refused to listen to his plans. They were silly plans, she considered, but she could have refused nicely, let him down gently . . . She waited for him to mention them again but he had nothing to say on the subject; he saw her and the cats into the flat, declined her offer of coffee with friendly casualness, and drove off. Not a word about meeting her again. She told herself that that was just what she wanted; she was sick and tired of him turning up at all hours and demanding coffee . . . That this wasn't in the least true didn't bother her; she wasn't in the mood to feel well disposed towards him.

'I hope I never see him again,' she told the cats, happily

unaware that fate was about to take a hand in her affairs.

Physio was busier than usual in the morning and, besides, there were several more patients on the wards to be treated, but other than her usual morning session with little Rita, Claribel was kept in the department. Mrs Green had gone to Out-patients, and Miss Flute had gone to the orthopaedic wards to accompany Mr van Borsele's round. Claribel worked her way steadily through a variety of broken limbs, frozen shoulders and arthritic knees while Tilly and Pat, at the far end of the department, dealt with an enormously stout and heavy man learning to walk after a severely fractured leg.

Claribel, bidding goodbye to a tough young man with a torn knee ligament, heaved a sigh of relief; Miss Flute would be back in another ten minutes and so would Mrs Green, unless Mr van Borsele chose to be extra long-winded; they would take it in turns to have their coffee and get their breath before working on until their lunch break. Mrs Snow, still cheerfully unable to use her arm as she should, was her next patient. She came trotting in, chatty as ever, and began peeling off the various garments she still found necessary despite the fact that it was quite a warm day and summer was well advanced. But presently, with her felt hat still firmly on her head, she sat down, put her arm on the cushioned table and settled for a cosy chat while Claribel took her through her exercises. She was in the middle of a saga concerning the neighbour's daughter and her goings-on when Claribel caught a movement out of the corner of her eye. Pat and Tilly were disappearing through the far door, suporting their patient to the waiting ambulance; the movement had come from the other end. She turned to look sideways to the waiting-room in time to see a man stoop to put a carrier bag between the benches.

'Just a tick,' she begged Mrs Snow, then hurried into the waiting-room, but the man had disappeared and there was no one else there. The bag was, though, wedged so that she couldn't get at it. Someone leaving something quite harmless for a patient who had perhaps not yet arrived? One of the workmen around the hospital leaving tools for later on? Or a bomb?

It seemed a bit silly to telephone the porter's lodge; perhaps she was over-reacting, and she was going to look an awful fool if it turned out to be someone's shopping. All the same, she explained to Begg, the head porter, and asked if he would notify whoever ought to know.

Mr van Borsele, head and shoulders thrust though the lodge's small window, writing a note to his registrar, looked up at Begg's worried, 'Does it look like a bomb, Miss Brown?'

He removed his head and shoulders and went to stand by Begg. 'Trouble?' he asked without any appearance of anxiety.

'There's Miss Brown, down in physio, says she glimpsed a man go into the waiting-room and leave a parcel. She went to investigate and can't move it. It's a plastic shopping bag; she says it's wedged tightly, and should anyone be told?'

Mr van Borsele took the phone from him. 'Claribel? Have you any patients there with you? One? Get out, both of you, as fast as you can. It may be nothing at all to worry about, but let us take precautions. Warn anyone nearby to get well clear. I'll see that the right people know. Now leave, fast.'

'Begg, give the alarm then get the police; you know the drill.' Mr van Borsele was already disappearing at a rippling pace through the hospital entrance. Once outside

he ran; the physiotherapy department was to one side of the
hospital, built on to one wing. He went to the far door and
saw Claribel, hurrying Mrs Snow towards him . . .

Claribel had wasted no time; Marc had sounded urgent
but unflurried. She had shot back to Mrs Snow, sitting at
her ease, with her shoes off, in order to ease her corns.

'We have to leave at once, Mrs Snow,' she had said as
calmly as she could. 'There's a suspicious parcel in the
waiting-room.' She had no need to explain; everyone knew
about bombs in plastic bags these days. 'We must be
quick . . .'

Mrs Snow had bent to her shoes. 'Oh, if you say so,
ducks. You'll 'ave ter wait while I get my feet back in,
though.'

Claribel had caught up the various garments scattered
around her patient. 'Never mind putting them on,' she had
said urgently. 'We can do that outside.'

Her voice had been drowned by the hospital alarm
sounding the pre-arranged signal in case of dire emergency,
and at the same time she had seen Mr van Borsele racing
towards them.

He was within feet of them when the bomb went off, so
that she didn't hear his roared warning to get down. She
wasn't sure, thinking about it later, if it was the explosion or
Mr van Borsele's considerable weight on top of her and Mrs
Snow which knocked the breath from her and left her head
spinning. It seemed to her that the entire hospital was
disintegrating about them, although, since the bomb had
been a small one, it was only the physiotherapy department
which was torn apart, subsiding into piles of debris. By
some miracle they escaped the worst of it. True, lumps of
ceiling plaster, torn and twisted equipment, tattered

remnants of curtains and broken chairs and stools and
landed on them, but their effect had been deadened by the
burst pillows from the couches which had more or less
smothered them.

Mr van Borsele rose cautiously to his feet, his beautiful
suit covered by feathers, bundles of curtain bits and a great
deal of plaster. He was rather pale but his voice was calm.
'Let's get out of here, shall we?'

He pulled Claribel to her feet and put an arm around her.
She was white and dazed and all she wanted to do was to
cling to him and bury her head in his shoulder. 'Hold hard,'
he told her in a matter-of-fact voice, and stopped to help
Mrs Snow to her feet.

'Me 'at,' said Mrs Snow urgently, 'and me shoes! Drat
them blessed bombs.'

Given some chance she would have searched for them but
Mr van Borsele said firmly, 'Out of here, as quick as you
can,' and caught her by the arm and urged her over the
rubble towards the further door.

Clarible was feeling peculiar; she had lost her shoes and
there was a warm trickle of something down one leg; she
had a fearful headache and all she really wanted to do was to
lie down somewhere and go to sleep. She muttered such
wishes aloud, to be answered by Mr van Borsele's, 'Later.
Let's get you outside first.' He added sternly, 'And do
remember that we have a patient with us.'

'Heartless brute,' Claribel mumbled, but she stumbled
along beside him, half listening to the rumblings and
grumblings of the ruin around her as it settled.

She became aware that there were other people around
them. Deft hands reached out to help them and she was
dimly aware of Mrs Snow's indignant voice going on about

her hat. Mr van Borsele's voice, unhurried and quiet, penetrating her dimmed wits. 'Mrs Snow, tomorrow I promise I will gladly call upon you and take you to buy a hat and shoes. You are a very plucky lady; I'm proud to know you.'

At this point Claribel was regrettably sick, and was conscious of Mr van Borsele's firm hand on her forehead. 'I bet you're not so proud to know me,' she said loudly, and hardly noticed when he picked her up and laid her on one of the trolleys being rushed from the accident room.

She was dimly aware once more of people doing things, but their voices were far away and she couldn't be bothered to open her eyes and look at them while they peeled off her clothes, cleaned her up, examined the long scratch on one leg and warded her. She slept soundly once she had been put to bed and, being young and strong, when she woke up some hours later she felt perfectly all right.

'I'll go home,' she told the nurse who came to look at her. 'You must be busy enough and there is nothing wrong with me.'

'I'll fetch Sister.' The nurse smiled at her and slid away and a moment later Sister came, and with her Mr van Borsele, looking immaculate, not a hair out of place.

He stood looking down at her. 'Feeling better? I'm afraid I knocked all the wind out of you. You want to go to your flat? There's no reason why you shouldn't but be good enough to stay quietly there tomorrow, in bed if you wish. Miss Flute asked me to tell you that she'll be round to see how you are in the morning. Don't worry about coming to work—they are arranging to transfer the physio patients to Clem's and St Giles'.'

'No work,' she repeated. Despite her pale face she looked

quite beautiful sitting up in a theatre gown several sizes too large for her, her hair in a golden tangle. 'Oh. I suppose I'll go to either Clem's or St Giles' . . .'

He smiled. 'I believe the physio staff are to go on protracted leave.' His smiled widened and she stared up at him. 'So you'll be able to come to Holland with me after all, Claribel.'

She gaped at him, taken by surprise and conscious of Sister's interest. Before she could say anything, he said to that lady, 'Claribel has been invited to stay with a member of my family in Holland. It will be an ideal break for her—just what she needs now after this—er—upheaval.'

Claribel cast him a fulminating look which he returned with a bland smile. He had her cornered; to manage to explain to Sister was impossible and now, in less than no time, the entire hospital would know that she was going to Holland with him. Perhaps there would be no snide asides; he was respected and liked and the general opinion was the he was a widower. He was aware of this surmise and had never chosen to correct it. Now the hospital grapevine would conclude that he intended to take a wife, and who better than Claribel Brown, who was a nice girl anyway?

She watched him go with a smouldering eye while Sister tripped along beside him, dying to spread the news.

Angry tears filled her eyes, but she brushed them away as Miss Flute came briskly down the ward and stopped beside her bed.

'Pat has gone to your flat to get you some clothes, dear. You are sure you feel all right? You had a very bad shock.'

'It was rather. Miss Flute, were there many people hurt, and is the damage bad?'

'Half a dozen with cuts and bruises—a miracle that there

wasn't more damage. Physio's wiped out though.' She repeated what Mr van Borsele had already said and added, 'They don't want us at Clem's or St Giles', at least not for some weeks—they plan to put up a temporary extension for us. Our place will have to be re-built and equipped of course—it will take months.'

She patted Claribel on the shoulder. 'We're to have paid leave for at least a month; by then they will have sorted things out. I'm coming to see how you are in the morning, so don't go rushing around, there's a dear girl. We found your bag, or rather the remains of it. Pat took your keys; she'll be along soon.'

'Is Mrs Snow all right?'

'She was taken to the accident room and given a check-up and then driven home. She was keen to know if you were all right and was full of Mr van Borsele's promise that he would buy her a hat and shoes. What a kind man he is, and so resourceful.' She glanced at Claribel's face. 'Well, I'll be off home; everyone's settled down again. There's a frightful mess outside, of course, but the hospital itself is back to normal. They're looking for the man; the police want to see you after you get to the flat. Will you be all right?'

Claribel nodded and Miss Flute left.

Pat came up with her clothes very shortly afterwards. Claribel dressed and, with Sister as an escort went down to the entrance. Almost there she said hesitantly, 'I think I'd better have a taxi, Sister, if someone could phone for one?'

'No need, you are being taken home, my dear.'

They had reached the entrance hall and Claribel saw Mr van Borsele sitting on a windowsill, reading a newspaper. He folded it up, put if away and came to meet them. 'Quite ready?' he asked in a voice nicely balanced between casual and concerned.

She stopped beside him. 'Yes, but I'm quite able to go home in a taxi . . .'

'I'm sure you are, but the police want to interview you and I think it might be a good idea if someone from this hospital was there as well.'

She stood undecided. 'Oh, I hadn't thought of that.'

Sister said firmly, 'You go along with Mr van Borsele, dear—he is quite right, someone ought to be with you.'

Claribel said, 'Yes, Sister,' meekly and got just as meekly into the Rolls. To tell the truth, she still felt not quite herself and the idea of having to answer a host of questions filled her with quite unreasoning fright.

Mr van Borsele didn't utter a word as he drove her to Meadow Road. When they reached the flat he took her key from her, opened the door, urged her inside and then followed her. The cats rushed to meet them and she bent to stroke them, and then sat down quickly because she felt giddy.

Mr van Borsele had gone at once to put on the kettle and, still without speaking, he fed the cats, made the tea and brought her a cup. She took it with a hand which she was ashamed to see still shook a little, which made her so cross she said snappily, 'It doesn't seem to have bothered you at all, being bombed.'

He said mildly, 'Well, you know, men aren't supposed to show their feelings on these regrettable occasions.' He added with a smile, 'I was scared stiff.'

Her peevishness dissolved. 'Oh, were you? No one would have known.' And then, 'How much do you weigh?'

'Very nearly fifteen stones. I hope I didn't hurt you too much.' He sat opposite her, very much at his ease, sipping his tea.

She shook her head. 'Heaven knows what would have happened to us if you actually hadn't protected us. I—I haven't thanked you, but I do, with all my heart.' To cover up a sudden shyness she added, 'Mrs Snow was marvellous . . .'

'Ah, yes. We have a date for tomorrow, she and I.' He put down his cup. 'The police will be here in an hour. Go and take a bath, Claribel, and get into your nightie and dressing-gown while I make some sandwiches for our supper. The moment they have gone you'll get into bed and stay there, and don't get up tomorrow until I've been to see how you are.' And, at her look, 'Delayed shock,' he observed smoothly.

It was easier to do as he said than argue with him. The bath soothed her; she washed her hair, too, and presently went back into the sitting-room. Mr van Borsele glanced up, his look impersonal. 'Good. I'm going to go next door for a few minutes. If I let the good lady know a little of what has happened there'll be no speculation among the neighbours.'

He disappeared and she sat down to finish drying her hair. She felt much better and her headache was bearable now. Enoch and Toots came to sit by her, pleased because she was home early.

'What shall I do?' she enquired of them. 'I expect we'd all better go home until something is arranged. I suppose someone will let me know . . .'

Mr van Borsele came back looking amused. 'I like the old lady next door. She will, of course, spread the tale far and wide; you'll not lack for neighbourly interest. She was concerned about you being alone tonight, but I was able to set her mind at rest. I would prefer to stay here myself, but that would hardly do, would it? So I've arranged for Tilly to sleep here. I'll fetch her in a while and collect her in the morning.'

Claribel said a little wildly, 'But there's no bed. I'll be quite all right, really I will.'

'Yes, I know that. She'll bring a sleeping bag with her and bedding; and don't argue, please, Claribel.'

She said weakly, 'But how will you manage on your own?'

'I've boiled an egg before now, and if I know Tilly there won't be any need for me to do even that.' He went through to the bedroom and came back with a brush. 'The police will be here shortly. May I use your phone?'

He talked for a few minutes to his registrar and then put the receiver back. 'I phoned your mother,' he observed, 'but I expect you'd like a word with her.'

She felt guilty. 'Oh, thank you, Marc. I should have thought of that—I feel awful about it.'

'No need. You see, you were badly shocked. I'll get your home now; there is time before the police arrive.'

He came across the room with the phone. 'Your mother was very upset,' she was told as she picked up the receiver.

She forced herself to be her normally matter-of-fact self and was relieved to hear both her mother and her father relaxing as she talked. When she had finished, Mr van Borsele said, 'Good girl. It's worse for them; they'll feel better now you have talked to them.'

The police arrived then to take a statement, a quite unfrightening business done over more cups of tea, and when they had gone Mr van Borsele fetched the sandwiches, went out to his car and came back with a bottle under his arm. 'Claret,' he remarked. 'Just what you need. I'm going to fetch Tilly in half an hour or so, but shall we talk first?'

'What about?' asked Claribel as, very nearly restored to normality, she bit into an apple and a cheese sandwich.

'You had a number of reasons why you shouldn't accompany me to Holland. None of them exist any more. On the contrary, a brief holiday is just what you want. I'm going back on Friday. I'll drive you down to Tisbury tomorrow evening and you can take the cats and leave them there while you are in Holland. I'm sure Miss Flute will help you pack tomorrow before the evening.'

Claribel stared at him, her mouth full of sandwich. She gobbled hastily before she spluttered, 'Well, of all the . . . I never did!'

'Neither of which remarks is to the point,' he observed calmly. 'Just for once can you not argue, Claribel; just accept my invitation gracefully.'

'You're only asking me because of Irma, though I don't see that it makes a scrap of difference if I'm with you or not.'

'I must admit that your company should give her the *coup de grâce*, for I shall make no secret of your going with me and the wretched girl seems to have ears and eyes everywhere. I must add, though, that I shall enjoy your company, although you won't see much of me; indeed, I dare say I shall be away for most of the time.' He added silkily, 'But, of course, you won't mind that, will you?'

He got up and washed their supper things, saw to the cats, made sure that the windows were closed and picked up his bag. 'Goodnight, Claribel. I'll go and fetch Tilly and I won't come in when I bring her back. Will you let me have your key? I'll see her safely in. You go to bed; she won't disturb you.'

He dropped a kiss on top of her golden hair and went away before she had framed a single word.

After a few minutes she got up and wandered around the little room. He had taken it for granted that she would do as he suggested and if she hadn't known that it was for his own ends, she might have been glad to accept.

'I won't go,' she told the cats, and got into bed, prepared to think the thing out in peace and quiet. She fell asleep at once and never heard Tilly creeping soft-footed around the living-room, arranging her makeshift bed.

Claribel slept soundly and indeed didn't waken until Tilly brought her a cup of tea. She sat up in bed, feeling quite herself again, and declared her intention of getting up and cooking their breakfast. 'And thank you very much for spending the night here,' she added. 'I didn't hear you come in. I only hope you weren't too uncomfortable.'

'Not a bit of it, miss. Jus' you 'ave yer bath and dress while I get us a bite ter eat.' Tilly nodded her head quite severely, standing small and round, arms across her ample bosom. 'The boss said as 'ow I was ter cherish you, and that I'll do.' At the door she turned to ask. 'These 'ere cats, shall I feed 'em?'

They had had their breakfast and were washing up together when Mr van Borsele arrived. His laconic, 'OK this morning?' wasn't quite what she had expected, but she was aware of shame at having expected anything else; she hadn't been hurt, only frightened, and here he was, immaculate as always, looking as though he had slept for at least twelve hours and never been near a bomb in his life. She was getting very sorry for herself, which wouldn't do at all. And he had been kind and thoughtful . . .

She said brightly, 'I had a marvellous night. Thank you for letting Tilly stay, it was nice having company.'

He nodded. 'Miss Flute will be coming presently. I'm going to run Tilly home now. I'll be here about six o'clock. Pack enough to see you through a couple of weeks in Holland; I doubt if there will be time to come back here on Friday while you pick over your wardrobe.'

She began, 'I don't . . .' and then stopped. It would be pointless to argue; he was doing exactly what he wished to do and if she raised objections she had no doubt that he would ride rough-shod over them.

When he and Tilly had gone she made another pot of tea and sat down to consider her immediate future. It was largely in the hands of Mr van Borsele and, thinking about it, she decided that a holiday would be rather nice anyway, even if Granny was an old tartar, which was more than likely if she and her grandson were alike. He had said that he would see very little of her and after all there was no need. The idea was for her to go to Holland with him in order to convince Irma that she might as well give up pursuing him. She had no doubt that he would find some means of letting the girl know that they were going and give her the opportunity of actually seeing them leave the country if she had a mind to do so.

She drank the rest of the tea, and the began to get the flat ready for her departure. When Miss Flute came they emptied the pantry, handed the old lady next door the perishable food that was in it, and then started to pack.

'I have no idea what to take,' declared Claribel pettishly.

'Wear that nice suit—that knitted one you bought; you can travel in it and wear it every day if you've a mind.

A couple of jersey dresses; skirts, blouses and jumpers; and take that nice blazer you had last summer. Oh, and a pretty dress in case you go out in the evening—two, perhaps?'

'I don't even know where I am going . . .'

'What fun,' declared Miss Flute. 'I wish I was in your shoes.'

'Are you going away, Miss Flute?'

'To my sister's in Cornwall. We shall be notified when they've got something planned for us, but that will be a couple of weeks at least. They have Mr van Borsele's address so they can reach you wherever you are.'

Claribel paused in folding her blouses. 'Miss Flute, do you think I'm a bit mad to go?'

'Not in the least. I understand from Mr van Borsele that you are doing him a favour in doing so, and the change of scene is just what you need.'

They sat down to a snack lunch presently and Claribel was very tempted to tell Miss Flute all about Irma, but it wasn't her problem and Mr van Borsele was known to be a reserved man who seldom allowed details of his private life to emerge. All the same she thought she would tell her mother . . .

Strangely enough it was Mr van Borsele who suggested just that as they drove to Tisbury. 'We have nothing to hide,' he observed coolly. 'I may say I think you have been making a great fuss over nothing, Claribel.'

'Fuss? Fuss! I haven't been fussy at all. I've agreed to your hare-brained schemes like a half-wit.'

He said soothingly to infuriate her, 'Now, now, don't malign yourself, Claribel. I have never thought of you as half-witted.'

'I should jolly well hope not! If I'd known what I was

letting myself in for . . .'

He chose to misunderstand her. 'Oh, you'll enjoy your stay with Granny.' There was no way in which she could ruffle his complacency.

'I shall take Mother's advice; probably she will tell me not to go to Holland.'

'As to that, we have to wait and see, don't we?' Then suddenly he wasn't mocking any more. 'Don't worry, my dear. Let life happen; don't try to alter it.' He sounded kind and reassuring; she found herself relaxing. Perhaps she had been making mountains out of molehills after all.

CHAPTER EIGHT

RATHER to Claribel's surprise, when they arrived at her home, Marc showed no sign of wishing to hurry away. Instead, when her father suggested that they might go to his study so that he might be shown a rare hand-drawn map of the village, he agreed with alacrity, so that she, rather at a loss, followed her mother into the kitchen to help with the supper.

'He can stay the night if he wants to,' observed her mother, prodding the potatoes.

Claribel had been so wrapped up in her own problems she hadn't thought about that. 'Oh—well, I expect he's going to his sister. I didn't ask.'

Her mother shot her a quick look; it was obvious that her daughter had a lot on her mind and moreover it apparently had nothing to do with the bomb. That had been exclaimed over and talked about at some length, and as far as she could see Claribel, once over the shock, had recovered nicely. It had been a very nasty thing to happen. She spoke her thoughts out loud, 'What a good thing Mr van Borsele was there.'

Claribel paused on her way to the dining-room with the plates. 'Yes, well, you see he was with the porter when I phoned—I did tell you.'

'I forget so easily, love.' A remark Claribel took with a pinch of salt; her mother never forgot anything.

When she went back into the kitchen the men were there, whisky glasses in their hands, and her father was pouring the best sherry into two more glasses for her mother and her. 'There you are, darling. Marc will stay to supper; he can't drive all the way back to London without a meal.'

Claribel put her tray down on the table. 'Do you mean to tell me,' she asked in a high voice, 'that you have to go back this evening? It's well after nine o'clock.'

He returned her icy green stare with a look of such innocence that she almost laughed. 'I enjoy driving at night,' he said placidly, 'and something smells delicious.'

Mrs Brown beamed at him. 'Watercress soup, my own make,' she told him happily, 'bacon and egg pie, and baked apples and cream for afters.'

Claribel, feeling that she was in the dark about something but not sure what it was, began cutting bread at the table. She very nearly dropped the knife when her father said, 'It really is most kind of you to invite Clari—a short break after that most upsetting incident is just what she needs.' He turned to smile at her amazed face. 'You'll enjoy it, my dear, won't you?'

The villian, she thought furiously, going behind my back and settling everything. She swallowed rage and said flatly, 'I expect I shall. I don't even know where I'm going.' She shot Mr van Borsele a look to burn him up, if that had been possible.

'Surprises are always nice,' he said smoothly, 'but I'll tell you. My home is in Friesland, the northern province of the Netherlands; still unspoilt, mostly farmland and lakes. The peace and quiet will do you good.' His voice was silky. 'You are rather uptight, only to be expected after your unpleasant experience.'

Her parents nodded approvingly and she turned away from his mocking gaze, aware that he was enjoying himself. Well, she wouldn't give him the pleasure of seeing how angry she was. 'It sounds delightful.' She spoke sweetly, although it was an effort. It would have pleased her mightily to have thrown the loaf at his head.

The talk was general during supper, ranging from bomb outrages to the Frisian landscape, the easiest routes to Holland, and vague, very vague, replies on Mr van Borsele's part to Mrs Brown's gentle questions about his life. It was almost eleven o'clock when he left with the assurance that he would be back at the end of the week to fetch Claribel.

They were standing in the hall and she said tartly, 'And what about Irma? Will you be able to find another girl to take out while I'm here?'

'Tut, tut,' he reproved her in a kindly tone to set her teeth on edge. 'You're being peevish. If it makes you any happier I shall be at the hospital each evening. There's a good deal of work still to do and this bomb has thrown the theatre lists rather out of line. Mr Shutter and I will be operating each evening; very awkward for all concerned, but the only solution. If I should see our friend Irma I shall tell her that you and I will be travelling together to Holland.' He bent and kissed her quickly. 'Don't worry, Claribel, no one shall take your place.'

'Much I should care. And another thing.' She was whispering, for her parents were in the drawing-room and the door was half open. 'How dared you go behind my back and tell Mother and Father about—about us? I haven't said I'll go with you . . .'

'Oh, yes you did. I expect this bomb business has curdled

your wits a little.' He gave her a wide smile and went out to his car and, without looking back, drove away.

Claribel shut the door with something of a snap, wishing that just once she might have the last word. 'I shan't go,' she muttered, all the while knowing that, of course, she would. It would be interesting to see his home, even if he wasn't going to be there for most of the time. She hoped that he would drive back carefully . . .

The few days passed peacefully. The weather was pleasantly warm, even if it was chilly towards evening. She combed through her wardrobe and got her father to take her and her mother into Salisbury so that she might add to it. She found just what she wanted: a pale blue pencil-slim wool skirt, a matching top in cashmere and a loose light cardigan, edged with satin ribbon, all more than she intended to spend. However, as her mother pointed out, good clothes were more economical because they looked good until they fell apart. Uplifted by this sensible remark, Claribel bought a short-sleeved silk dress which exactly matched her eyes, and which would, as she was careful to point out to her mother, come in very useful. Mrs Brown agreed; any dress likely to catch Marc's eye and increase his interest in Claribel would be useful. Claribel had thought exactly the same thing, though, of course, she didn't say so. Indeed she wasn't actually conscious of thinking it.

Mr van Borsele arrived shortly after lunch on the Friday, accepting coffee from Mrs Brown, enquiring casually after Claribel's health, passed the time of day with her father and signified his intention of leaving as soon as she was ready.

'We'll look in at my flat as we go,' he told her. 'Tilly will have my bags ready. We're going from Harwich. I went to Meadow Road, by the way, and talked to your neighbour;

she'll keep an eye on your place while you're away. Miss Flute sends her love; she's off today as well. They're still clearing rubble away at Jerome's; it will be some time before they have put up temporary buildings and there's almost all the equipment to install.'

Claribel, looking very pretty in the knitted outfit, went to say goodbye to her cats and collect her overnight bag. She felt excited now; she had tried to drum up some ill feeling against Marc during the week, but somehow it had been difficult. He had behaved very badly, but he had been kind, too, and he had undoubtedly saved her from injury when the bomb had exploded. She told herself that she owed him something for that; by the time she came back to England Irma would have tired of him and she would have paid off her debt to him.

She said goodbye to her mother and father and got into the car, reflecting as she did so that it was surprisingly easy to get used to comfort and luxury—travelling in a Rolls Royce, for instance.

Mr van Borsele had gone back to speak to her father and she wondered why; he had already said goodbye. Whatever it was was briefly spoken, then he got in beside her and they drove away.

He had nothing to say; she peeped sideways at his profile and found it a little stern. Perhaps he was thinking about the patients he had operated upon during the week, or the work waiting for him in Holland. She searched her head for something to say, but, since she couldn't think of anything, stayed silent, too.

Presently he broke the silence. 'We'll stop for tea at Oakley. Is there any need for you to do anything at the flat?'

'No. If you're in a hurry there's no need for us to

go there.'

'Not as hurried as all that. We'll just check that everything is all right there, and we'll have a meal at my flat; we don't need to get to Harwich until round about ten o'clock.'

She was a little puzzled; he sounded friendly enough, but somehow remote. Perhaps he was regretting his invitation. She was a level-headed girl but given to impulsive acts upon occasion. 'If you're having second thoughts, do say so,' she begged him. 'You can drop me off at the flat and I can catch a train in the morning.'

He gave a crack of laughter. 'Claribel, you're letting your imagination run riot again. Here we are at the end of a most successful campaign to shake off Irma and you suddenly choose to behave like a teenager who doesn't know her own mind.' He added bracingly, 'You, a grown woman of twenty-eight, with a mind of your own.'

'There's no need to bring my age into it,' said Claribel crossly. 'I only wondered.'

Just for a moment he put a hand over hers. 'Just remember that I'm glad to have you with me.'

Which was reassuring. On the other hand, of course he was glad; she was a necessary buffer between him and the wretched Irma. If the girl got her claws into him, he would get what he deserved. She was ashamed of the thought the moment it had flitted through her head, and she frowned, trying to understand why she thought of him in such a muddled way. They had started off on the wrong foot, of course . . .

Meadow Road looked dingier than ever in the afternoon sunshine, and her flat, even with its brave show of flowers in the tubs and its cheerfully painted door, looked shabby. They went inside together, checking that everything was as it should be, and as they left, a few minutes later, Claribel wondered how she would feel when she returned to it. London, that part of London anyway, seemed at that moment the worst possible place in which to live.

That couldn't be applied to Marc's flat, she admitted to herself as he ushered her through its dignified entrance. No neighbours peered through grubby net curtains as they went in and, with the door shut, no noise from the street spoilt the quiet.

Tilly had been on the look out for them. She had the door open as they reached it. "'Ere you are then,' she exclaimed cheerfully. 'I got a nice tasty meal all ready. Just you tidy yerselves up, the pair of yer, while I dishes up.' She turned away to go back to the kitchen, saying as she went, 'An I've packed yer things like you asked, an' that young woman 'oo's always pestering you, she rang up, wanted to know where you were.'

'What did you tell her?' asked Mr van Borsele.

'Like yer says—out of town and leaving for 'olland this evening.'

'Good girl. What a treasure you are, Tilly.'

'Go on with yer.' She gave him a wide smile and went.

Sipping her sherry in his beautiful sitting-room, Claribel observed, 'Well, that's the last of Irma. I don't really need . . .' She caught his eye. 'Oh, well, I suppose just to be on the safe side.' She frowned. 'But do you have to tell her so much?'

'Dear girl, just think for a moment. Do you not remember as a child being forbidden something you wanted very much and for that very reason wanting it all the more, and if by some chance it was available to you, you lost all interest? The same idea applies very roughly to the tiresome Irma.'

They dined deliciously with Tilly trotting in and out, making sure that they ate what she put before them. As she put a magnificent Bavarian cream on the table by way of dessert she admonished them to eat it up. 'For it's something I don't fancy, meself, not with me figure being what it is. But it'll do you good, the pair of yer; yer need to keep plenty of flesh on them big bones of yours, sir, and as for you, miss, another ounce or so won't 'urt them nice curves.' A speech which caused Mr van Borsele to smile and Claribel to blush.

He had timed their journey very well; the bulk of the passengers were already on board and the queue of cars waiting was a short one. Mr van Borsele sat back in his seat, his eyes half closed, so it was all the more surprising when he said in a tone of satisfaction, 'I have been hoping that she would come.'

Claribel sat up straight. 'Irma—she's here? She's not going to Holland, too?'

'Ah, no, I think not. Merely making sure that we are, together. Try and look a little loving if you can, Claribel.'

Claribel arranged her features into what she hoped was a suitably moony rapturous expression, and just in time. Irma rapped on the window and Marc lowered it. There were two men with her, both looking sheepish, as well they might, thought Claribel, beaming with false sweetness at Irma's face peering at them both.

'You meant it,' she cried. 'You really are going away. You're not married?'

'Not yet.' Mr van Borsele sounded patiently civil. 'But

take my word for it, it won't be very long now.' He smiled at Claribel, his dark eyes gleaming with amusement. 'Just as soon as arrangements can be made. Isn't that so, darling?'

Just as well be hanged for a sheep as a lamb, thought Claribel and heard her voice, revoltingly gushing, 'Yes, dear.' She turned the gush on Irma. 'You would be so surprised at what a lot there is to do even for a quiet wedding.'

Irma said huffily, 'I shall have a big wedding with bridemaids and a train and dozens of presents.'

'Why, of course,' agreed Claribel sweetly, 'but Marc and I aren't exactly young, you know, we're rather past all that.' She looked ahead and exclaimed, 'Oh, look, we're going aboard at last. Goodbye, Irma. When you marry do let us know; you'll make a lovely bride.'

Mr van Borsele turned a snorting chuckle into a cough. 'Yes, do do that,' he urged and started the car. 'Enjoy your drive back. London or Bath?'

'Oh, London now, but I suppose I might as well go home tomorrow.'

He swept the car onto the ship's car deck and Claribel took the smirk off her face. 'Now that is the last time,' she declared.

'I hope so. I must say you were superb, Claribel. Had you ever thought of going on to the stage? You know, just for a moment I quite believed that you were looking foward to our wedding . . .'

It was a pity that the business of parking the car and getting out of it interrupted the white-hot remark ready on her tongue. When they met in the bar later after going to their cabins he silenced her with a bland, 'I do think you were rather severe about our approaching middle age,

Claribel. Maybe you feel your years, but I can't say that I feel all that elderly.' He sat her down at a table. 'A drink before we part for the night? I hear it's quite choppy out at sea; a brandy might be a good idea for you.'

She said strongly, 'What a perfectly horrid thing to say. And I hate brandy.'

'If I apologise handsomely, will you please have the brandy?'

He could be charming when he wanted. She said rather ungraciously, 'Oh, well, all right,' and, when her glass had been put before her, sipped at it. It warmed her nicely and she sat back and look around her.

The ferry was fairly full. There were a good many people milling around laughing and talking and she asked, 'Do you always come this way?'

'Usually; it gives me a night's sleep. Sometimes I fly, but that means I haven't got the car and have to rent one. I use the hovercraft occasionally.'

'Don't you want to stay in one place—your home?'

'Frequently.'

It was obvious that she wasn't going to make much progress in that direction. She realised that she didn't know where he lived. In the morning she would ask him, but not now. She tried a different approach. 'How did you find Tilly? She is a dear, but not a bit like a housekeeper.'

'She was a patient of mine some years ago. I had just bought the flat and she told me one day that she hadn't got a job, her husband had died and she had no family, no one who mattered at any rate. So she has been housekeeping for me ever since. You like her?'

'Very much. I expect she looks after you beautifully.'

'Indeed she does. Are you sleepy, Claribel?'

'No, not in the least.'

'You've never asked me where I live. Are you not interested? I have of course told your mother and father. Either you are very naïve or you have a touching trust in me.'

She said gravely, 'Well, I do trust you, and you said you lived in the north somewhere. But I don't know much about you, do I? I know that you have a sister . . .'

'Three sisters—the other two are married and live in Holland; they're all a good deal younger than I. There are aunts and uncles and cousins, too, scattered around but my grandmother is the only member of the family I see frequently. She lives in Leeuwarden but I live in a small village to the south of the city. The motorway to the south is close enough to be able to drive down to Amsterdam, about ninety miles away—I go there once a week to operate. I go to The Hague, too—that is a hundred and twenty miles—but I do most of the work in Leeuwarden and Groningen. I have beds in the hospitals there, and consulting rooms.'

'You aren't at home very often. Do—do you live alone?'

He didn't smile but his eyes gleamed with amusement. 'Yes. I have a housekeeper and her husband sees to the garden and the odd jobs and in fact looks after things when I'm away.' He did smile then. 'Now you know all about me, Claribel.'

'Yes. Thank you for telling me."

'You are entitled to know. Are we not friends?'

She nodded. 'I'll go to bed, I think. Where do we meet in the morning?'

'I've asked the stewardess to bring you tea and toast when she wakes you—we'll stop for breakfast on the way. I'll knock on your door just before we get in.'

She got to her feet and he got up with her. 'Goodnight, Marc.' She was taken by surprise when he bent to kiss her cheek. 'So hard to break a habit,' he murmured.

She had been remarkably silly, she thought drowsily. She had agreed to everything he had suggested without finding out how long she was to stay with his grandmother. A few days? A week? Longer? As far as she could see there was no reason why she shouldn't go back to England within a day or so. Irma, having seen them actually board the ferry, would most certainly have gone back to Bath, and she would be able to go back home until the hospital had got something sorted out . . . Her thoughts became more and more muddled and she fell asleep in the middle of them.

She slept all night; if the crossing had been rough the brandy must have acted as a splendid soporific. As she ate her toast and drank her tea she hurried to dress, and she was just ready when Mr van Borsele knocked on the door.

She called him to come in, wished him a friendly good morning and collected up her gloves and handbag. 'Are we there?'

'About ten minutes to go. Come on deck and take a look.'

It was a fine morning, but cool. The Hook lay before them, surprisingly busy for that early hour, and Claribel looked around her with interest. It looked, rather to her disappointment, rather like any English port but there wasn't much time to inspect it for car owners were asked to rejoin their cars.

Going ashore proved both brisk and easy; they were waved past the last official and Mr van Borsele took the road north. They were on the main road almost immediately, bypassing Delft, racing along until they were almost at Amsterdam and then changing to the Alkmaar road. Half-way there, Marc pulled in to a petrol station.

'We can get breakfast here,' he told her and left the car to be filled up as they crossed to a small café, with flagpoles before it and neat gingham curtains. It was just as neat inside, with tablecloths to match the curtains and a great many pot plants on the windowsills. They sat at a window and the café owner brought them coffee and a basket of rolls and croissants, thinly sliced cheese and ham, boiled eggs and small pots of jam in a dish.

Claribel, who was famished by now, enjoyed every morsel and presently, much refreshed, they got back into the Rolls.

'Is it much further?' she asked.

'Over the dyke and then about twenty-five miles.'

'Where's the dyke?'

'A good thirty miles from here and then the dyke—that is about sixteen miles. We shall be at my grandmother's in about an hour.'

He had been a pleasant companion as they drove, pointing out anything which he thought might interest her, answering her questions patiently, and now, on a cross-country road, he was at pains to tell her something about Leeuwarden. Not a very big city, he assured her, but with some beautiful old houses and any number of peaceful little streets if one knew how to find them.

They reached the Afsluitdijk, the high sea dyke on one side of the wide road, the Ijsselmeer on the other, and raced across it, and presently Claribel could see the land ahead of her: Friesland, Marc's home.

On the mainland they joined the main road again although when they reached Franeker Marc turned off and drove quite slowly through the town so that she might glimpse the narrow gabled houses by the canal and take a quick look at the *Gementehuis*—Dutch Renaissance at its best, he pointed out. 'And the Planetarium is close by. Perhaps you will have the chance to come and see it while you are here; it is unique: the man who built it, Eise Eisinga, worked each evening by candlelight—it took him seven years.'

'I wish I understood Dutch,' sighed Claribel, suddenly apprehensive.

'No need—almost everyone speaks or understands a little English. Besides, we speak Fries among ourselves.'

'Oh—like the Welsh speak Welsh?'

'Exactly. Here is Leeuwarden.'

The outskirts were sober middle-class red-brick houses, each with a small garden, but soon they gave way to shops and old houses leaning against each other in a mass of small streets.

Marc had turned away from the heart of the city and presently joined a street lined with large houses set behind high walls or glimpsed through gardens, well away from the street. Half-way along he drove between gateposts and along a short semi-circle of gravel, and stopped before a fair-sized house with a flattened gable, a very large front door reached by a double pair of steps, and three rows of large windows. There were trees encircling it and formal flower beds cut into a pattern, which extended as far as the high wall shielding it from the street.

Mr van Borsele got out to open Claribel's door and they reached the steps just as the door was opened and a white-haired man greeted them.

'Domus—Granny's butler; been with her man and boy,

and runs the place.' Mr van Borsele clapped the old man on the back very gently. 'Domus, this is Miss Claribel Brown.'

Claribel shook hands and smiled and was ushered into the hall, long and narrow and lofty, its walls almost covered by paintings and with an outsize chandelier hanging from the ceiling. Mr van Borsele had a firm grip on her arm and Domus went ahead of them to open arched double doors.

It was a very large room with enormous windows draped in red velvet and a good deal of large furniture, too. The lady who came to meet them across the polished floor suited her surroundings very well: she was tall and rather stout, with a very straight back; Claribel was reminded of Queen Mary, King George the Fifth's wife. The hairstyle was the same, too, and the rather severe expression . . . her heart sank. But only for a moment. Marc's hand slid from her elbow to take her hand in his while he flung the other arm round the old lady. 'Grandmother, my dear . . .' He bent to kiss her. 'Here is Claribel, as I promised.' He pulled Claribel gently forward. 'Claribel, this is my grandmother, Baroness van Borsele.'

Claribel and the old lady shook hands; they were of a similar height and surveyed each other gravely, each liking what she saw. 'Dear child,' murmured the baroness, 'such a pretty name and such a pretty girl. I am so delighted to have you here. I lead a very quiet life, you know, but we will contrive to give you some amusement and it will be delightful for me to practise my English.'

Claribel murmured something; the old lady's English was every bit as good as her own; there was only the hint of an accent, just as Marc had.

'Let us sit down and drink our coffee. Marc, you will stay to lunch?'

'Thank you, Grandmother, but I must go home this afternoon, there's a good deal of work waiting for me.'

'Of course, my dear.' His grandmother had seated herself in a tall chair by one of the wide windows. 'Such a pity that we shan't see more of you, but to have a glimpse of you is delightful. I only hope that you don't work too hard.'

He said casually, 'I enjoy my work, my dear.' He had seated himself opposite Claribel. 'You will actually have a peaceful time here, Claribel, with no patients to worry about and no one to remind you of Jerome's.'

She said doubtfully. 'Don't you come here? To operate in the hospital, I mean?'

'Indeed I do. I shall be in Leeuwarden tomorrow, but I shall be too busy to come here. A good thing,' he added blandly. 'As I have just said, there will be no one to remind you of Jerome's.'

She was nonplussed. 'Oh, yes, of course, and naturally you have your friends to see.' There was a faint waspishness about her voice.

'That, too, but don't worry, I'll let you know when we're going back, and you can always phone me. The hospital has this address so that you will be in touch with them.'

She took a sip of coffee, feeling that she needed it badly. She hadn't expected to see him every day but she had supposed that they would have spent some time together; now she realised that he had no intention of doing anything of the sort. He had indeed told her when he had first suggested the whole thing that she wouldn't have to see much of him, but she hadn't taken him seriously; now she saw that she should have done. He had invited her to Holland for exactly the reason he had told her in the first place: to get rid of Irma once and for all. As usual, he had arranged things to suit himself. She gave him a charming smile while her eyes flashed green temper at him. 'How nicely you have arranged everything. I'm sure I'm going to love being here.' She turned to her hostess. 'It is so kind of you to invite me, Baroness.'

The old lady has been sitting quietly listening to Marc and chuckling silently; the girl was delightful, and capable of managing her much-loved grandson, and yet, she was sure, unaware of his real purpose in bringing her to stay with her. He had always had his own way, never arrogant about it, just silently going ahead with what he intended to do, listening politely to advice and ignoring it for the most part, looking after his sisters in an unobtrusive manner until they married, ignoring their hints that he should get himself a wife. But here was someone he would listen to . . . She smiled kindly at Claribel. 'My dear, I believe that we are going to have a most enjoyable time together. There is a great deal to see in Leeuwarden and we can drive out to the surrounding country, too. Domus shall drive us.'

Claribel smiled with suitable enthusiasm and reflected that she would much prefer Marc to drive her, and then felt mean at the thought. Sensibly she applied herself to giving civil answers to the baroness's questions while Mr van Borsele sat back in his chair looking amused.

Domus came in presently, addressing himself to the lady of the house and then he turned to say something to Marc. When he had gone, Claribel said diffidently, 'Why did he call you Baron? Aren't you just mister?'

'Er, no, but I don't bother with that in England. Domus is rather a stickler for titles and so on. I hope you don't mind.'

'Mind? Why should I mind?' She had gone rather pink

and both grandmother and grandson studied her appreciatively; she looked quite lovely when she was put out about something. 'I mean,' she added with chilly politeness, anxious not to be rude, 'it really doesn't matter, does it?'

'Not in the least.'

Domus came in again and murmured briefly and the baroness said briskly, 'Lunch is ready. I arranged for it to be served early, Marc, for I know you are anxious to get back to your own home.'

A remark which gave Claribel a distinctly forlorn feeling.

They lunched in a room at the back of the house, overlooking a surprisingly large garden laid out with shrubs and trees and with a small fountain at its centre. The table was covered by a thick white damask cloth and the silver was heavy and old. Claribel, eating soufflé off Delft china, wondered briefly what Marc had thought of the Woolworth's mugs from which he had drunk his coffee at her flat. Besides the soufflé there were cold meats on a big silver dish and side dishes of salad, and more coffee afterwards.

Marc got up to go very shortly after they had finished their meal, kissed his grandmother, patted Claribel on a shoulder in a casual manner, saying carelessly that he would doubtless see her at some time or other, and took himself off.

'Such a dear boy,' said his grandmother as they stood at the window watching the car disappear down the drive. Claribel didn't say anything; she was struggling with an overwhelming sense of disappointment.

Any qualms she might have had about being welcome in the baroness's house were quickly dispelled; she was cosseted from the moment she woke each morning until she went to bed at night. Her hostess, despite her eighty-one years, carried her age lightly; the pair of them went sightseeing each day, driving at a stately pace with Domus at the wheel. Claribel and her kind hostess visited Franeker, Dokkum and the northern coast, taking narrow country roads so that she could see the villages and the prosperous farms, all built to the same pattern, the house in front, connected to a large barn by a narrow neck, the whole mostly thatched over red tiles. She had the dykes explained to her, too: the dead dykes, no longer needed because the land had been reclaimed from the sea; the sleepers, the dreamers and, nearest the sea, the watchers. In time, the baroness explained, as more and more land was reclaimed, a sleeper became dead, and they all moved back one. The villages, few and small near the coast, were mostly built along the dykes, small neat houses, too, with tiled roofs with strings of washing in their back gardens. So different from her own home but, in its way, just as peaceful and charming.

She explored the city, too, while her hostess rested after their lunch: strolling round the shops, gazing at the Weigh House, poking her pretty nose down narrow streets and going to the museums. The Frisian Museum was, to her mind, easily the best with its lovely old costumes and jewellery and the collossal sword of Grote Pier who had driven away the Saxons four hundred years earlier. Frisians, she had discovered, were large people, both men and women, but he must have been a giant among them.

It was on her fourth morning there that the baroness suggested that she might like to go off on her own. 'I have business to attend to,' she explained, 'and it is too nice weather for you to stay indoors.'

So Claribel wandered off into the centre of the city, not sure what she wanted to do. The days so far had been delightful, for there had been various friends and relations calling at the house, as well as their daily excursions, but right at the back of her mind was the thought that Marc had made no effort to see her. He had phoned, so his grandmother told her, but to all intents and purposes he had removed himself to the other side of the world. She told herself that she didn't mind in the least; he was a tiresome man, always wanting his own way and getting it, too. All the same, she missed him.

She went and leaned on the railings by the Weigh House, staring at nothing, wondering why she felt so dispirited. Perhaps she shouldn't have come, but then Irma might have made herself troublesome.

'Hello, Claribel,' said Marc from behind her, and she spun round to face him, suddenly alight with happiness—a lovely feeling, she thought bemusedly, like going out of doors very early on a summer morning or going home after a hard week's work and opening the kitchen door and seeing her mother—a lovely complete feeling in which content and delight and joy were nicely mixed.

He stared at her for a long moment. 'Pleased to see me?' he asked.

'Yes, oh, yes.' And then, aware of his intent gaze, 'I'm having a simply lovely time with your grandmother.'

'Good. I've given myself a day off. Would you like to see my home? We'll go back and have coffee if you will with Grandmother first, and then go on home for lunch.'

She nodded her head slowly, her hair golden in the sunshine. She wanted very much to go to his home for lunch; she knew with a suddenness she didn't try to understand that she wanted to go to his home and stay there. How could she not have known all these weeks that she loved him?

He stood quietly before her, smiling a little, his hands in his pockets, impeccably dressed as always only this time slacks and a tweed jacket replaced his more sober suits. His dark eyes were intent, watching her face. He must have found his scrutiny satisfactory for he observed softly, 'Well, well,' and then, 'Shall we go?'

They had their coffee on the veranda at the back of the house, and the regimented rows of flowers glowed in the sunlight.

'Charming, isn't it?' observed the baroness, 'but of course I'm old-fashioned enough to like a formal garden.' She glanced at Marc. 'Will you dine here, my dear?'

'Thank you, Grandmother, yes.' He looked across at Claribel. 'Ready? Shall we go?'

She had said very little while they had been sitting there, doing her best to breath normally so that her heart would stop its frantic thumping against her ribs, but she was finding it difficult. She had tried not to look at Marc, either, but once or twice his dark eyes had caught and held hers and she had had difficulty in looking away. She would have to do better than this, she told herself; the very idea of him discovering that she was in love with him made her feel quite ill. After all the fuss she had made about helping him in the first place . . .

They said goodbye and she got into the car beside him and, intent on being exactly as usual, embarked on a flow of small talk, something so unlike her usual manner that Marc, agreeing to her platitudes with every sign of interest, hid his amusement.

CHAPTER NINE

THEIR way lay through the city and then, once free of the suburbs, Marc left the main road south for a narrow country road running between water meadows, each with its quota of cows. Claribel admired the cows, the flat meadows and the occasional farm, keeping up a steady stream of small talk which really needed no answer, hardly pausing between one topic and the next for fear that there would be silence between them. Her tongue was in danger of cleaving to the roof of her mouth by the time Marc turned on to a narrow bricked road on top of a dead dyke. There were trees ahead and the glimpse of red roofs. Seeing them, she asked, 'Are we nearly there?' and heaved such a sigh of relief that Marc smothered a laugh.

'The village is behind those trees; I live just beyond. In a moment you will see the lake. There are a series of them; this particular one is at the end.'

He sounded just as usual and she decided that she had panicked for no reason; she would have to get a hold of herself. It wouldn't be for long now; soon she would be going back home and as soon as she could she would get another job. Somewhere where she would never see him again . . . She sighed again and Marc allowed himself a quick smile.

The village was small but compact, encircling a red brick church, very severe in appearance, but there were trees and pretty little gardens before the small houses and a shop or two. There were people about, too, housewives, and children playing in the street, and solid men going about their business. They saluted Marc as he drove by and he lifted a hand in reply.

'They all know you,' observed Claribel brightly.

'Well, we were all born here.' He had turned a corner by the church and slowed into a lane leading away from the village towards the lake. The trees were thicker here and presently there was a high iron railing with a vast lawn behind it and, in the centre, a castle. A small castle, but a castle nevertheless, complete with pepperpot towers, and a big double door, flanked by tall narrow windows.

'Oh, look,' cried Claribel, 'what a darling little castle. Does someone live there? I wonder . . .' She paused. 'It's yours, isn't it?'

'Yes.' He swept the car between high wrought-iron gates and up the drive, straight as a ruler, to his front door.

I don't know the first thing about him, thought Claribel miserably. He was just a consultant surgeon with a short temper and a liking for coffee in London, but here he's something quite different . . . She got out of the car reluctantly when he opened her door. 'You might have told me,' she said.

'Why? What difference would it have made? Don't be a silly girl and come inside.'

He took a bunch of keys from his pocket, unlocked the massive double doors and propelled her forward into a lobby which in turn opened on to a square hall, across the floor of which came a thin, elderly man with a solemn face. As he reached them he spoke to Marc in a reproachful way and shook his head. Marc laughed and clapped him on the shoulders. When he spoke it was in English.

'Warmolt, this is Miss Claribel Brown, from England.'

He bowed his elderly head and, when she put out a hand, shook it. 'Welcome, Miss Brown. We are pleased that you come.' He smiled widely and didn't look solemn at all. 'I'll fetch Sieke.'

'His wife and my housekeeper. Do come into the drawing-room meanwhile.'

She had a quick look round her as she went. The floor was paved with black and white marble and had a lovely old carpet down its centre. The walls were white plaster, hung with paintings, and the staircase was at the back of the hall, solid oak with a carved balustrade and dividing halfway up into two wings leading to a gallery above the hall.

Marc had opened an arched door and was waiting patiently for her. She went past him into a very large room with french windows opening on to a veranda at the side of the house and a row of small windows at the front. Its high ceiling was plaster with pendant bosses and the chimney-piece was an elaborate two-tier dome, ornately carved. There were a number of handsome cabinets against its walls, displaying a vast quantity of silver, glass and porcelain, and there was a beautiful console table under the windows, which was curtained with old rose brocade, held back by great tasselled ropes. The chimney-piece was flanked by two William and Mary settees and on each side of the console table were a pair of eighteenth-century armchairs of gilded wood and covered with tapestry. But there were more modern pieces as well: wing-back armchairs, a ladies' worktable with its silk bag, lamp tables with a handsome commode with a serpentine front bearing a Delft bowl filled with flowers.

'Oh, how very beautiful,' exclaimed Claribel, rotating slowly so that she wouldn't miss anything. 'And lived in, too.'

'Hence the mixture of its furnishings—each generation adds something. And it's certainly lived in.'

As if to underline his words the door was pushed open and two bull terriers came darting in, going first to Marc and then to Claribel, to stand politely while she admired them and stroked their smooth heads.

She said shyly, 'I liked your flat in London, but this is your real home, isn't it?'

'I was born here, and I hope I shall die here. Here is Sieke; she will take you upstairs. When you come down we'll have a drink.'

Following the housekeeper, a stout woman with a nice friendly face, Claribel was led out of the room and up the staircase, to be shown into a charming room at the front of the house. Castle or no, it lacked none of the comforts and luxuries of the twentieth century; there was a bed of some pale wood, covered by a quilted spread, its rose-covered satin made to match the curtains at the two windows, between which was a sofa table with a triple mirror upon it. There were easy chairs, too, and a table or two and a roomy mirrored wall closet. And the bathroom adjoining it was just as luxurious. Claribel sat down before the mirror and tidied her hair and powdered her pretty nose and made a mental list of topics she could talk about with Marc; she must remember to be friendly but not too eager—a few well-chosen questions about the castle and its history, but she mustn't get too interested either. She went back downstairs, well primed, dreading and at the same time longing to be with Marc; the day stretched before her, probably full of pitfalls, but, after all, she had been alone with him on a number of occasions during the past few weeks . . . She would have to pretend that nothing had altered.

Only when she got to the bottom of the staircase did she become aware of voices in the drawing-room, and when she went in it was to find that she need not have got into such a fidget; the room was full of people. Well, not full, but there were seven people standing around Marc with drinks in their hands. He came to meet her.

'There you are, Claribel. I thought you would like to meet some of my friends at lunch. Come and be introduced.'

Four men about Marc's age and three younger women; they had strange-sounding Friese names like Sjamke, and Waltsjer, and they at once enveloped her in warm friendliness, laughingly pronouncing their names for her, explaining who was married to whom and who were merely engaged, asking her how she was enjoying herself. At lunch she sat between Marc and a slightly older man called Wobberen who it seemed, was a doctor with a practice in Dokkum and who knew London well, so that there was a great deal to talk about.

The table was large and round, gleaming with silver and glasses and everyone talked to everyone else while they ate cold salmon and a salad which looked too good to eat and then a Dutch apple tart with lashings of whipped cream. They had their coffee at the table, served by Warmolt, grave as a judge, going silently about the room; he suited his surroundings very well, Claribel decided, for the dining-room was as grand in its way as the drawing-room, with panelled walls and a great deal of strapwork on the ceiling.

It was well past three o'clock when Marc's guests went

their various ways. He stood on his doorstep with Claribel beside him, seeing them off, and when the last car had gone to took her arm.

'Like to look round the grounds?' Not waiting for an answer, he walked her round the side of the castle along a narrow path with the castle walls on one side and a gentle grass slope on the other. 'There was a moat a very long time ago,' he explained.

There were sweeping lawns at the back of the castle and a knot garden, as well as a lily pond with goldfish, but there were no formal flower beds here. Instead there were flowering shrubs, great banks of roses and a lavender hedge bordering a grey flagged path which led them to a circular bed of colourful annuals. And, beyond that, trees and an expanse of parkland.

'Oh, it's beautiful,' cried Claribel. 'How can you bear to leave it?'

'Ah, but I come back to it, you see. It has been here for a very long time; it is ageless and timeless.'

He tucked her hand under his arm as they strolled along, and Claribel suffered a succession of what felt like electric shocks and tried not to notice them.

'I've a letter for you,' he went on, 'from Jerome's. Remind me to let you have it when we get back indoors.' Sooner than she had wished.

Warmolt, pacing in a stately fashion towards them, caused them to stop and wait for him. He bowed politely to Claribel, who felt that she should bow back, and addressed himself to Marc.

Whatever it was engendered a brief conversation before Marc observed, 'An aunt and uncle have called. We had better go back.' He said something to Warmolt who quickened his pace ahead of them. 'Tea,' said Marc, 'and light conversation.'

The two people waiting for them in the drawing-room were middle-aged, tall and inclined to stoutness; the man had the aggressive nose Claribel had rightly associated with the van Borseles. They greeted her kindly, made small talk over tea and biscuits and, in due course, went away. Claribel liked them both but although they were van Borseles she had been unable to pronouce their names. Not that it mattered; she wasn't likely to meet them again. The thought saddened her and at the same time reminded her that Marc had a letter from the hospital. He gave it to her when she asked.

'I'll go upstairs and change and you can read it while I'm gone,' he observed cheerfully.

They had got things sorted out at Jerome's. She could transfer to a hospital in the north of the city until such time as a new physiotherapy department could be built and equipped, or, if she wished, she could be released from her contract with Jerome's and find her own work.

It would have to be the latter, she decided immediately. For one thing the new hospital was too far away from her flat for her to be able to get to and fro within a reasonable time each day, and, far more importantly, she needed to be free to find a job wherever she wished. And that, she told herself decisively, was as far from Marc as possible.

She had pulled herself together by now and when he came back, elegant in one of his dark suits, she was able to tell him of the contents of the letter. 'It couldn't be better, she told him. 'Just the chance I wanted to make a change.'

He nodded calmly. 'Then this is splendid news for you. I shall be going back in four days' time. There will be no need for you to answer the letter; you will be able to see them in person.'

'So I shall,' said Claribel. With the upheaval her feelings had undergone she hadn't given much thought to returning. The awful finality of it paled her cheeks, something which Marc noted with interest.

He said smoothly, 'I shall miss my visits to Meadow Road—that is, unless you plan to stay there?'

'I've no idea where I shall be,' Claribel said with a snap. She added recklessly, 'I'm told there are plenty of jobs in Australia and New Zealand.'

'Must you go quite so far?' asked Marc blandly. 'One doesn't need to run to the ends of the earth, you know.'

Oh, but one does, thought Claribel unhappily, and even that wouldn't be far enough away for her to forget him. She said rather too effusively, 'What a delightful day I have had; I liked your friends—and your aunt and uncle.'

'Splendid. We had better go now or we will arrive too late at Grandmother's. Have you any plans for your last few days here?'

She began at once on a recital, thought up on the spur of the moment, of the multitude of things she intended to do. 'Your grandmother is taking me to Dokkum again and she has kindly offered the car so that we can to to Groningen, only it may be too far for her to go. And then I have to buy presents to take home and—and go up the Oldehove Tower . . .'

They were in the car driving back to Leeuwarden, the dogs sitting side by side on the back seat. She had wished Sieke and Warmolt goodbye and taken a last look at the little castle, wishing with all her heart that she could have explored it; it was so perfect. She had felt the warmth of the generations of van Borseles who have lived there; no sinister corners or creepy passages, just an abiding contentment and happiness.

She said dreamily, 'It is a very beautiful castle; I'll never forget it.' She added quickly, in case he might think that she was too interested, 'Leeuwarden is a delightful place too . . .'

'You like heights?' asked Marc idly. 'The Oldehove Tower is quite high. It leans a bit, too, although there is a lift. The view from the top is quite something.'

She hated heights and she disliked lifts but she had just told him with enthusiasm that she was going to the top of the tower. She said airily, 'Oh, good, I'm looking forward to it.'

Back at Baroness van Borsele's house, she went to her room to change her dress and shower. She chose to wear the dark blue crêpe-de-Chine, aware that it highlighted her hair and added sparkle to her eyes. She took great pains with her face and hair and was rewarded by a cursory glance from Marc which did nothing for her ego. And anyway, why was she bothering? she reflected, sipping her sherry with pleasure and listening to his grandmother's very informed history of his castle; Marc had never once given her the impression that he had any interest in her other than as a useful dispenser of coffee and a means of getting rid of Irma.

'And what did you think of the castle?' enquired the baroness as they sat at dinner. 'Is not the circular room in the central pepperpot tower quite charming? Marc's mother used it as her own sitting-room.'

'I didn't see it,' said Claribel flatly.

'You didn't take Claribel on a tour of inspection?'

'No, Grandmother.' He sounded pleasant enough but he wasn't going to say more than that.

'Quite a good thing,' said Claribel chattily. 'My head is crammed with so many museums and churches and farms, not to mention whole streets of lovely old gabled houses, I don't suppose it will hold another thing.'

'Ah, but you must make room for the Oldehove Tower. Remember to take your camera with you,' Marc observed. 'You should have some impressive photos to show around when you get back.'

She stole a look at him. She was reminded forcibly of the first time they had met; his face bore a similar expression of impatience and somehow his aggressive nose registered hauteur. He looked at her before she could turn her eyes away and she flushed under the gaze from the black eyes boring into hers.

He left shortly after dinner. 'I've a list in the morning and a teaching round in the afternoon, but I dare say I'll see you before we go.' He kissed his grandmother and took Claribel's arm. 'Come and open the door for me,' he suggested. 'It will save Domus's feet.'

But when they reached the great door and she put out a hand to lift the massive latch he lifted it off. 'Have you any idea why I asked you to spend the day with me?' he asked her.

She thought about it for a moment. 'Well, I expect you thought that I might like to meet some people—and I did enjoy that, really I did. And it was nice to see your home . . .'

He nodded. 'I imagined that was what you might have thought. And you found my home, er, nice?'

She looked up at him. 'I found it enchanting. Quite

perfect inside—as far as I could see—and out. Anyone who is fortunate enough to live in such a heavenly place . . .' She drew a long breath. 'You must be very happy there.'

'I am. And I intend to share my happiness with a wife and children.'

She went a little pale but she was composed enough. 'I'm glad. I'll think of you being happy there.'

He smiled a little. 'And where will you be, Claribel?'

How easy it was to tell lies when one was desperate. 'I've decided to go to New Zealand. Mother has cousins there.'

'You will leave broken hearts behind you.'

She gave him a questioning look.

'Enoch and Toots. You can hardly take them with you.'

She didn't know what she had expected him to say, certainly not that. A faint forlorn hope buried deep inside her finally died. 'They'll be happy with my mother.'

She bent to pat the two dogs standing patiently at their master's heels. 'These two are awfully good—you must miss them when you're away from home.'

He opened the door. 'It occurs to me that we are having a quite inane conversation about nothing at all, Claribel. Goodnight. I'll be in touch.'

A horrid end to a day which hadn't been as wonderful as she had hoped.

She was a sensible girl, even if her heart was in a thousand pieces. She spent the next two days being driven around the surrounding country with her hostess; Sneek and Bolsward, with its lovely old churches and town hall, the lakes where they stopped to drink coffee or tea, and Hindeloopen where Claribel bought some of the famous painted wooden bowls and spoons. She left the baroness in the car here at that lady's urging, and strolled along the sea wall to see the 'Gossip Bench' where the old men of the little town spent their leisure, looking out to sea and talking among themselves. On the third day they went to Groningen, where they had lunch at the Crémaillère Restaurant and took a slow stroll past the university.

During the last day of all she packed her things, spent the morning with the baroness and then, at her suggestion, decided to go out for a walk. There had been no word from Marc other than a brief telephone conversation. They would leave on the following day, he told her, directly after breakfast, and get back to London some time during the late afternoon. 'And be sure and let your people know,' he warned her.

She sensed that he had no time to talk at length, so she agreed without quibbling and rang off. She had, she supposed, served her purpose, and then she chided herself for self-pity. She had had a lovely holiday and never for one single moment had he led her to suppose that he was even faintly interested in her.

It was a dull, warm afternoon, and she had bought her presents; there was still Oldehove Tower to visit. She told the baroness where she was going, promised to be back for four o'clock tea, and took herself off.

The tower was truly massive. She walked all round it and then, together with several other tourists, took the lift to the top. Now that she was actually doing it, she was sorry that she had been silly enough to show such enthusiasm about it. If it hadn't been for Marc she would have backed out, but some misguided pride had made her go ahead with it. The lift was small and full of people and she stood in the centre which kept the awful feeling of being shut in at bay. She got out at the top with a feeling of enormous relief which turned at once to dry-mouthed panic.

The view was indeed magnificent; everybody else was hanging over the railings pointing out landmarks and taking photos. There were a number of children, too, dashing to and fro, and several well-meaning sightseers who, with the kindliest intentions, urged her to go to the rails and look over too. To escape their puzzled glances when she shook her head, she walked cautiously to the other side, taking care not to look at the panorama below her. Thank heaven they would all go back presently and she with them. She wished there was some sort of seat but, since there wasn't, put a hand on the wall and stared at the stones. They were comfortingly solid under her hand—like Marc, impatient, wanting his own way, annoyingly monosyllabic at times, able to live in luxury and choosing to work all hours in hospital theatres, but, just like the wall, solid and dependable.

She made the mistake of looking around her and closed her eyes again. She would have to rejoin the other tourists; she could hear them laughing and talking. Someone put a head round the corner and called out to her in a cheerful voice. She waved and actually smiled and the head disappeared. At least she would be able to tell Marc that she had been to the top of Oldehove Tower. She started back, careful not to look towards the railings, but when she reached the lift door she found it closed. What was more, when she pressed the knob at the side nothing happened. They had all gone; she would have to wait until they were on the ground floor and get the lift back. She would hate going down alone but perhaps there would be other people coming up . . . Nothing happened when she pressed the knob a second time and then, after a few moments, a third time. It struck her that perhaps the head which appeared round the corner had said something to her, had even been telling her something vital about the lift . . .

She waited for a few minutes before trying to open the lift doors and then she went to the head of the staircase. it snaked away from her into a gloomy pit into which the narrow steps disappeared. There was no rail and it wound, as so many staircases did, in a spiral round a central pillar.

She made a tentative movement to descend and then withdrew her foot, in the grip of quite illogical panic. She had always hated heights but now she realised that she was acrophobic, a condition which had nothing to do with being cowardly, something she couldn't help. Clinging to the wall, she stepped back from the stairs, shaking with fright. Until somebody came back with the lift she was powerless to do anything. She edged herself up against the wall feeling sick.

The baroness looked up from her embroidery frame as Marc entered the drawing-room of her home. He greeted her with affection, refused tea and asked, 'Where is Claribel? I managed to get finished earlier than I expected. I thought she might like to explore the castle before we have dinner with you.'

The old lady snipped a silk thread. 'Well, dear, she went for a last walk through the city and intended to go to the top of Oldehove . . .'

'Has she been gone long?'

'Rather longer than I expected. She said that she would be sure and return for tea and it is now well past that hour.'

He stirred restlessly. 'I think I'll go and see if she is still there.'

'Yes, my dear. Such a dear girl, and so right for you.' She looked over her glasses at him. 'She is, isn't she? Or am I wrong?'

He smiled and bent to kiss her cheek. 'Grandmother, you are so right. I cannot imagine living a day longer than I must without her.'

'Run along then, dear. Don't bother to come back here until this evening—I'll put dinner back half an hour; that will give you plenty of time.' And, at his raised eyebrows, 'To propose, dear.'

Claribel had retreated as far as possible from the edge of the tower, with her back to the central wall, leaning so hard against it that she might have been trying to bore her way into its thickness. She was cold and still literally scared stiff, so that moving even a hand was an effort of will. She had given up wondering what to do; surely sooner or later the lift would return and until then she could only remain still. It was a good thing that she didn't know that the face which had addressed her had told her that the lift was out of order and that everyone was walking down . . .

She kept her eyes steadily on the wall and to keep up her very low spirits she began to recite all the poetry she could call to mind. Marc, climbing the stairs fast, was taken aback to hear her rather shaky voice: ' "It is the little rift within the lute, That by and by will make the music mute." '

'As I live and breath,' muttered Marc, taking the last few stairs at a gallop, 'she is reciting Tennyson.'

She had her eyes shut but she opened them at the sound of his feet. She stared at him wordlessly and he plucked her from the wall and held her fast.

It was too much. She burst into tears. 'I'm the most frightful coward,' she sobbed into his shoulder and tried very hard to stop weeping. Any moment now he would make one of his laconic remarks to deflate her, as though she wasn't already deflated enough . . .

'My poor darling girl.' His voice was tender with a hint of laughter in it. 'Never mind, I'm here now, you're quite safe. Didn't anyone tell you that the lift had broken down?'

She mumbled into his shirt front and he stroked her bright hair. 'I can't go down those awful stairs—I go all stiff. Oh, Marc . . .'

'My darling love, of course you will go down them, behind me, and you will be quite safe, and you need never go higher than the pepperpot towers in the castle for the rest of your life.' He put a gentle hand under her chin and kissed her very slowly. He said, 'We're going to be married, you know, and live happily ever after.'

'But you don't love me . . .'

'Oh, yes, I do, have done for a long time now; I've been waiting for you to discover that you love me, too—and you have only just done that, haven't you?'

She stared up at him. 'Well, yes—the other day you know, when you asked me to lunch and all those people came too.' She smiled shakily. 'I don't know what I would have done, trying to live without you.'

'Well, you're not going to live without me, my dearest, ever again. And now keep quiet while I kiss you.'

Presently Claribel drew away a little. 'I—I promised I'd be back for tea.'

'I called in and saw Grandmother; it was she who told me you were here. We'll go there for dinner but now we're going to my home—our home—so that you can poke that charming nose into every nook and cranny.'

He took her arm and started for the stairs. 'Stand behind me and put your hands on my shoulders and keep your eyes on the back of my head. You're quite safe, sweetheart.'

Love can be a very powerful feeling; if he had told her to jump over the railings she would probably have done so; as it was, she did as she was told, listening to his calm voice planning their journey back to England and their future.

On the bottom step he turned and took her in his arms. 'My brave girl. Stop shaking, darling, I have you safe and I don't intend to let you go.'

Claribel took a grip on herself. 'Don't you? Don't you really? You didn't just say—the things you said—to coax me down?' She looked up at him and saw the look in his eyes and added hastily, 'No, you didn't. I shouldn't have said that.' She reached up and kissed him and was kissed breathless in her turn.

'Why were you reciting Tennyson?' he asked, and tucked a lock of hair behind her ear.

'To take my mind off things.'

'He wrote about you, too—did you know? "Where Claribel low-lieth, the breezes pause and die." Only I'm not a breeze and I'm very much alive and in love with you.'

They smiled at one another and he kissed her once more, watched by a middle-aged couple who happened to be passing, a boy and the small dog with him. The couple sighed and linked arms, remembering their own youth, the dog barked, and the boy, in the manner of all boys, whistled rudely.

To Claribel, lost in bliss, he could have been a string orchestra playing 'Moonlight and Roses' under a perfect sky.

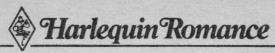

✦ Harlequin Romance

Coming Next Month

2935 TRUST IN LOVE Jeanne Allan
Fleeing from malicious, career-threatening rumors, successful model Kate returns to her small Nebraska hometown. There, unexpected help from onetime town rebel Ty Walker makes her stop running and fight back.

2936 PLAYING SAFE Claudia Jameson
Demetrius Knight disapproves of Grace Allinson—which suits her perfectly. After one heartbreak she has no desire to get involved again. Unfortunately his young sister's needs make it hard for Grace to befriend her while determinedly ignoring her brother!

2937 FEELINGS Margaret Mayo
Melissa, for good reasons, isn't interested in any man—much less someone like Benedict Burton, who demands that she scrap her adopted Miss Mouse appearance to be like the pretty, vivacious women he prefers!

2938 ONE-WOMAN MAN Sue Peters
Radio Deejay Berry Baker can't understand why her fund-raising plan for a children's ward at St. Luke's Hospital has turned into a contest for control—between herself and Julian Vyse, the senior medical consultant. But the battle lines are clearly drawn....

2939 MORNING GLORY Margaret Way
Someday young, talented Kit Lacey knows a man will come along to match her zest for life. And when Thorne Stratton, international news correspondent, arrives in Queensland's Eden Cove, he exactly fits the bill. Convincing him, Kit finds, is quite another matter.

2940 NEPTUNE'S DAUGHTER Anne Weale
Oliver Thornton is a name out of Laurian's past, and one she has every reason to hate. When Oliver turns up once more in her life, she's wary. Surely he will only break her heart—again!

Available in October wherever paperback books are sold, or through Harlequin Reader Service:

In the U.S.
901 Fuhrmann Blvd.
P.O. Box 1397
Buffalo, N.Y. 14240-1397

In Canada
P.O. Box 603
Fort Erie, Ontario
L2A 5X3

Temptation™

TEMPTATION WILL BE
EVEN HARDER TO RESIST...

In September, Temptation is presenting a sophisticated new
face to the world. A fresh look that truly brings Harlequin's
most intimate romances into focus.

What's more, all-time favorite authors Barbara Delinsky, Rita
Clay Estrada, Jayne Ann Krentz and Vicki Lewis Thompson
will join forces to help us celebrate. The result? A very special
quartet of Temptations...

- Four striking covers
- Four stellar authors
- Four sensual love stories
- Four variations on one spellbinding theme

All in one great month! Give in to Temptation in September.

Harlequin Superromance

**Here are the longer, more involving stories you
have been waiting for... Superromance.**

Modern, believable novels of love, full of the complex
joys and heartaches of real people.

Intriguing conflicts based on today's constantly
changing life-styles.

Four new titles every month.
Available wherever paperbacks are sold.

SUPER-1

ATTRACTIVE, SPACE SAVING BOOK RACK

Display your most prized novels on this handsome and sturdy book rack. The hand-rubbed walnut finish will blend into your library decor with quiet elegance, providing a practical organizer for your favorite hard-or soft-covered books.

Only $9.95

Approximately 16" x 8" when assembled

Assembles in seconds!

To order, rush your name, address and zip code, along with a check or money order for $10.70* ($9.95 plus 75¢ postage and handling) payable to *Harlequin Reader Service*:

Harlequin Reader Service
Book Rack Offer
901 Fuhrmann Blvd.
P.O. Box 1396
Buffalo, NY 14269-1396

Offer not available in Canada.

BKR-1A

*New York and Iowa residents add appropriate sales tax.

HARLEQUIN SIGNATURE EDITION

VIOLET WINSPEAR
HOUSE OF STORMS

Editorial secretary Debra Hartway travels to the Salvador family's rugged Cornish island home to work on Jack Salvador's latest book. Disturbing questions hang in the troubled air over Lovelis Island. What or who had caused the tragic death of Jack's young wife? Why did Jack stay away from the home and, more especially, the baby son he loved so well? And—why should Rodare, Jack's brother, who had proved himself a man of the highest integrity, constantly invade Debra's thoughts with such passionate, dark desires . . .?

Violet Winspear, who has written more than 65 romance novels translated worldwide into 18 languages, is one of Harlequin's best-loved and bestselling authors. HOUSE OF STORMS, her second title in the Harlequin Signature Edition program, is a full-length novel rich in romantic tradition and intriguingly spiced with an atmosphere of danger and mystery.

Watch for HOUSE OF STORMS—coming in October!

HOFS-1